ALONE TOGETHER

CRISTELLE COMBY

ALSO BY CRISTELLE COMBY

ALSO BY CRISTELLE COMBY

Short Stories

PERSONAL FAVOUR (*Neve & Egan* prequel)

REDEMPTION ROAD (*Vale Investigation* prequel)

The short stories are exclusively available on the author's website:

www.cristelle-comby.com/freebooks

Edition: 1

ISBN: 979-8592362576

Credits
Cover artist: Dienel96

CONTENTS

LAST CALL FOR ALL PASSENGERS

KILLIAN - 01 AUGUST

I couldn't miss it. I wouldn't miss it. It wouldn't do to be late. No, it simply wouldn't do at all.

All this had been going through my head since I glanced at my Nautilus *Patek Philippe* wristwatch. When it told me the time was 10:40, I cursed while a depressing realisation dawned on me. The monitor displaying the Geneva Airport's flight departure times wasn't early—I was late. This sort of lapse rarely ever happened to me. My job all but demanded timeliness, over and again; thus, understanding different time zones was something that I took considerable pride in. But this little upheaval threw me off my mental balance. Worse yet, my lateness was leaving me with an appalling lack of leverage.

The white letters in front of me silently advised that boarding had begun for Flight SWA 1528 at Gate A2—my flight. I felt anger turn to heat that rose inside my old, weary bones as I looked between the suitcase at my feet and the meandering queue stretching in front of the baggage disposal desks.

I only had minutes left to get to Gate A2. The lack of time and lengthy line made checking in luggage an impossible task. I turned on my heel and left the suitcase where it was. There was no other way. A sacrifice had to be made to make my flight.

Besides, what was in there to justify my keeping it? Nothing vital, only clothes and toiletries I could buy anew at any decent shopping centre. I could easily forward the bill to someone else for their replacement. Meanwhile, everything work-related was in my briefcase, including my laptop. Everything I actually cared about was in my pockets. So in the grand scheme of the universe, the suitcase was no great loss.

I ran all the way to the escalators to the upper floor and its central Security Gate. By the time I flashed my boarding pass at the fast-lane entrance machine, I was out of breath. When it opened, I hurried on through, not slowing when I came upon a family of Asian tourists sporting an assortment of neon-coloured shorts and T-shirts.

I squeezed in between them and their cabin luggage, moving to the front of the priority queue. Whatever come-backs they had for my rudeness were lost on me.

"Late," I said to the boyish man minding the metal detector. He gave me a disapproving gaze. He was not having one bit of it, not at all. It was a perfect mirror for my attitude towards my tardiness.

When his frown deepened at my words, I was surprised. Of all the airport security officers I'd encountered, I thought a Swiss one would understand. If there was anything I'd learned during my three-month stay in Lactose Country, it was that the Swiss were very big on punctuality.

At the end of my first month here, I emailed Head Office

a sizable report on the Geneva branch of the Blackfriars Bank they had sent me to audit. While the issues raised about our Swiss employees were many, timeliness was never one of them. Even though traffic was a nightmare in this waterside city—what with it being split into two halves by the Rhone River, only so many bridges to cross over and an extensive maze of one-way streets—they somehow always clocked in on time, and nor did they mind staying late in the evening if the workload required it of them. As a fellow man of professional aspirations, I admired this about them. But that admiration was not mutual in this case.

I threw my briefcase into the first available plastic tray before dashing through the metal detector. The damned thing beeped and the security officer stepped in front of me, blocking my path. I cursed, realising I'd forgotten to empty the contents of my pockets. When one is rushing, one does things that waste even more time, it seems.

"Keys? Telephone?" the man asked, his words heavily accented.

"Sorry, I forgot," I mumbled, my own vowels betraying my Scottish ancestry. I took a step back, tossed my phone and whatever else I had at the bottom of my trouser pockets into the nearest tray. After adding my watch to the top of the pile, I walked through again.

The man eyed me like a hawk every step of the way. What did he think? That I was an undercover terrorist? Since when had those camel-shepherds worn Tom Ford suits and Barker shoes?

When the detector remained silent this time, the officer stepped aside, dismissing me from his awareness while the Asian father took my place. I reclaimed my belongings, slipped the briefcase strap over my shoulder with the left hand while pushing everything else deep in my coat's pocket with the other. The whole time, my eyes were already busy scanning the path ahead, looking for signs of the gates' whereabouts.

When I couldn't find any, I walked forward at a rapid pace. Though my lungs protested the continued abuse, I pushed ahead. Rows of designer boutiques with their glossy floorboards and wooden display cases imprisoned me, forced me to rush along their inviting fronts until I was clear of them. On the other side, I found a large hub with a money exchange stand in the centre and a coffee shop at the back. If I'd had the time, I'd have stopped to grab some coffee.

I finally found what I was looking for: large monitors with departure boards standing high over the crowd. I scanned through them, finding Flight SWA 1528 on it, near the top of the list. It was still boarding.

A glance at a nearby clock revealed the time to now be 10:46. If the flight was on time, they would have closed the gate already. My love of punctuality aside, I thanked the stars I wasn't the only one running late today.

Now that I'd crossed Security and they'd scanned my boarding pass, there was still a chance. The computer system keeping track of the passengers' roster knew I was here and would alert the team minding the gate. Surely they wouldn't depart without at least calling out my name on the Tannoy. Near as I could tell, that hadn't happened yet.

I looked up, left and right, before *finally* finding the signs pointing to the various gates. I dashed the hallway leading to A2, praying that it wasn't at the other end of the airport.

A swarm of sweaty teenagers in matching athletic team

shirts stood on the moving walkway I stepped upon. They just stood there motionless, taking all the available space while chatting with each other or fiddling with their smartphones. Had I had the time for it, I would have smashed their heads together. This generation was so enamoured and babied by all this technology. I was sure none of them would survive a day out in the wilderness. I was no Luddite, mind. Human evolution had certainly marched in lockstep with improved technology. But losing touch with reality is no improvement at all.

I elbowed my way through teenagers Seven and Twelve, forcing my way forward while looking for more signs of my gate. If they said anything about bulling my way through, I didn't hear them. Another walkway, a sharp turn later and Gate A2 was in sight at last.

The whole way there, I cursed the secretary who'd arranged this trip. Bloody temp... Asking for professionalism from them was like asking a fish to climb Mt. Everest. If I missed my plane, I was going to make sure everyone who mattered knew whose fault it was. Stupid woman, telling me the flight was taking off at noon. Well, she may have been sitting comfortably at Head Office in London, but I sure as hell wasn't. And bloody Switzerland wasn't on GMT time either.

A thinning crowd of mismatched hoodies, jackets, suitcases and backpacks were already lined up in front of Gate A2. That was just perfect, wasn't it? What was the point of paying extra to go in before anyone else if you showed up at the last bloody second? I swore the minute I was wheels down in Stockholm, Head Office was going to get an earful about that temp.

A tall man with a round face said something in a foreign

tongue as I pushed past him to the head of the line. It sounded quite nasty. I couldn't have cared less.

"Business Class," I said over my shoulder, ticket and UK passport held up for emphasis.

My cheeks were on fire and I could feel a stream of sweat running between my shoulder blades. God, I couldn't wait to sit down and prop my feet up. I was tired of Switzerland, of its stuffy warm summer air and of the bloody heatwave it'd been stuck in for the past fortnight. Not that I was eager for another assignment so soon, but a change in temperature would be welcome.

"Oi! Mind the queue, mate," another man grumbled after I shoved him aside. I didn't spare him a second glance, never mind words. I was three feet from the gate desk and nothing was going to keep me from it now. I had an appointment in Sweden at 3pm that very afternoon. Unlike this flight, I had no intentions of being late for that. If Stockholm's branch of Blackfriars Bank was expected to be on its best behaviour for their audit's first day, so should their examiner.

The woman minding the gate pursed her plush lips while setting her thick auburn eyebrows in a frown. No way she couldn't have seen me part the crowd like the Red Sea in my mad scramble to her post. "Boarding pass and ID please," she requested, her voice making it clear that I'd better have had a good excuse for disrupting her corner of Geneva Airport.

I pushed both of the items into her hands, too out of breath to say anything. It was easy to pinpoint the exact moment her eyes caught the words "Business Class" on the boarding pass; her lips stretched into a practised smile. It figured. These people were trained to uphold a certain level of respect and esteem for those flying in the higher classes. It didn't say much about their self-respect but I accepted it.

Going with the flow meant enjoying the amenities that went with that.

"Thank you for choosing Swedish Airline, sir," she said as she scanned my boarding pass. As she waved me through, she added, "Have a pleasant flight."

2

LIGHTNING AND THUNDER

KILLIAN - 01 AUGUST

The clear blue skies of Switzerland turned a dark shade of grey as we flew over Germany. My thoughts drifted towards the land that lay beneath us. I guess what they say about Germans being hard workers was true. It was one of the few countries I'd never been sent to. Somehow, the two German offices of Blackfriars Bank had always met or exceeded their monthly goals, year after year. To be honest, it made me a tad bit jealous. I'd promised myself a visit to Germany one day, just to see how they did it.

The plane I was stuck in, an Airbus A220-100, was on the smaller end of the scale. It only had a carrying capacity of a hundred passengers or so. As a result, we were flying lower than the heavy carriers, straight into the mushy weather. It being such a small plane made me less than excited for the intense turbulence we were bound to feel. I preferred it when the company booked me on larger planes and their hulking, invincible frames for international flights. Besides, those flying giants came with all the comforts you could think of: movies, fine foods and drinks, blankets, toiletries.

Not only did this plane have none of those things, it wasn't particularly comfortable either. The only difference between Business and Economy was rows of two seats instead of the standard threes. Nothing like what I was used to on the larger overseas flights with their comfortable reclining seats.

Still, the warm, wet hand towel the stewardess handed me upon departure had been appreciated. Feeling the need to de-stress after my frantic chase through the Geneva terminal, I placed the wet towel on my forehead, tilting my head back.

A beep followed by the captain's voice cut through the silence. "Ladies and Gentlemen, this is your captain speaking. We hope you are enjoying your flight thus far and thank you for flying with us today. I do, however, have a bit of bad news. I'm sorry to say, but the weather in Scandinavia today isn't very good."

Well, at least that Swiss heatwave was behind me at last, I thought. That cheery revelation made me smile.

"There are several small storm formations over Sweden that we will have to cross through to reach Stockholm," the captain continued. "As a result, this flight may be a little rough, so I encourage all of you to remain seated at all times. And don't forget to keep your seatbelts on. Thank you." True to his word, the little seat-belt sign went on at the end of the captain's announcement.

Somewhere in the back of the cabin, a little child was crying. He or she had been doing that for the past ten minutes or so. I heaved a sigh as I felt a headache settling in. Business Class just wasn't what it used to be. Now there was no partition to separate us from the rest of the plane, only a flimsy curtain that did nothing to block the child's annoying wails.

Said curtain was an ugly shade of yellow, the same colour as the padding on the seats and headrests. That, coupled with the cobalt blue used for the carpet and the plastic of the seats, left little doubt as to this plane's origin. One only had to hope it hadn't been shipped straight out of an IKEA factory as a kit.

I was nursing my second glass of cheap on-board generic whiskey when heavy rain started beating down on the plane. I think we weren't far from Denmark by then. The further north we flew, the bigger the droplets grew. The sound of them hitting the fuselage became like hail beating down on a car roof.

It got to the point where the sight made me want to pee, which made me curse Mother Nature. By my estimation, we had to be flying well over Sweden by now. We'd hit the ground in twenty or thirty minutes max, so there was no point in subjecting myself to the tiny, unsanitary on-board facilities. I chose to hold on.

Another beep heralded the plane's speakers coming to life again. "Ladies and Gentlemen, I'm sorry to have to tell you that we will not be landing at Stockholm Arlanda Airport as planned."

The captain's words were followed by a general moan of disapproval that swallowed up the beginning of the next part of his announcement. "...is closed to all traffic due to severe bad weather in the east. We have requested to be diverted to Göteborg-Landvetter, but they are already taking all the heavy carriers diverting from Arlanda. Instead, we will be pushing north and landing in Kiruna Airport." Another louder set of disapproving moans rose in response, drowning out more of the captain's words. "...measures will be taken on the ground to ensure you can resume your journey as smoothly as possible.

On behalf of Swedish Airline, we apologise for this unforeseen turn of events, but we have to put our passengers' safety first."

By the time the speaker became silent once more, my groan had joined the chorus of the other passengers. Well, that was just lovely. First, I was late to board this damn plane. Now I'd be late to reach my destination too. If I were the type to believe in such idle things, I'd think the universe was trying to send me a message or something.

As soon as I could, I caught the attention of the young freckled stewardess tending to the Business Class. Her uniform was a national anthem in itself—blue pencil skirt, blue cotton jacket with yellow stripes, yellow scarf, and a blue hat. As she moved closer, she offered me a dimpled smile while asking me how she could be of help.

"Kiruna," I said. "Where the hell is that? Is it close to Stockholm?"

"I'm afraid not, sir." Her smile didn't waver as she delivered the bad news. "Lapland mining town, about a thousand kilometres north of Stockholm; not that far from the Norwegian Sea."

"You've got to be kidding me. Is there nothing closer? An empty highway, an abandoned field, a fuckin' golf course?"

Though my tone was harsh, she gave me a full-blown smile and a soft chuckle, like I'd just told her a joke. The whole thing felt unnatural and practised.

"I'm sorry, sir," she said, with a shrug of her shoulders. "I'm not the one at the helm." With another empty chuckle and a shake of her head, she moved back to the front of the plane.

Well, that just took the cake, didn't it? Was the universe really conspiring against me after all? Because if it was intent on making me miss my meeting, it had just succeeded. With literal flying colours. Wonderful.

My bladder was making a fresh call for my attention. I tore my safety belt off and got to my feet. I followed the young stewardess down the central aisle, aiming for the *cludgie* at the front of the plane.

"Sir, you should stay seated," she said.

"Need to use the *lavvy*," I nodded at my destination.

Her practised smile was back on and in full bloom while she shook her head. "Oh, I'm sorry, but the toilet in the front's out of order." She motioned to the partition behind me. "There's two more at the back of the plane."

That left me speechless. For once, I just didn't have the words to complain.

"Jesus, Mary, and Joseph, could this day get any bloody worse?" I muttered as I turned on my heel and flung the partition open.

My shoulders slumped when I caught sight of the queue near the back. Best I could tell, this plane was almost full of passengers. And thanks to the waterfall pouring outside, it was no surprise that a lot of them felt the same need I did.

I sighed but there was nothing for it. I started the long walk down the central aisle, hoping the line had moved an inch by the time I joined it. Midway there, we experienced a dip that could only be a momentary loss of altitude. I heard a few gasps coming from everybody and I had to grip the nearest headrest to stay upright.

That moment did clear up the line. Three people near the front of the queue thought better of it and went back to their seats. That only left a teenage boy waiting in front of the door. Both of his hands were grasping the overhead compartment for balance. *Maybe the universe wants to cut me a break after all*, I thought ruefully.

As I stood behind the boy, the left *lavvy* door opened so that a pale-faced middle-aged woman could come out. One of the stewardesses got up from the jump seat she'd been sitting on to help her get to her seat near the front.

After the kid went in, I took his place and waited for the person in the right lavatory to come out. Another jolt of turbulence suddenly hit us. It shook me up bad enough to make me reach a hand towards the overhead compartment.

The remaining stewardess motioned for me to get back to my seat, but I ignored her. If they were able to get up and help people back to their seats through these bumps, then I sure as hell was allowed to take a simple piss. *Ridiculous*, I thought, wondering if I could get Head Office to start booking with another airline after this.

Nonetheless, she was all but ready to sit up when the right door finally opened. I wasted no time rushing past the man who'd been using the facilities and shut the door behind me. *Relief!*

After I did what I'd come there to do, I washed my hands in the minuscule stainless-steel bowl that was optimistically called a "sink". I'd just shut off the water when a loud bang tore through the plane. The lights flickered just before the whole plane shook an instant later. No convenient hand-holds this time; I lost my balance to the point of hitting my back against the door. The door handle dug deep into my hip while the side of my head connected hard with the flimsy partition. Even though the space was too cramped up for me to lose my footing, I still had to grab the mini-sink to steady myself.

"This is the Captain speaking, we've just been hit by lightning. It shook us a little, but there's no reason to worry." While the voice on the intercom sounded tense, it didn't sound afraid, so no reason for me to be, bump or not. I got back to my feet, dried my hands and turned around to push down on the door handle.

"The rest of our journey is going to be a little bumpy as we're crossing through a turbulence area," the Captain continued as I exited the *lavvy*. "But we should reach Kiruna shortly. I am advising all passengers and cabin crew to remain seated with their seatbelts on for the rest of the journey."

I noticed straight away that the two stewardesses were gone from their jump seats at the back of the plane. A glance to my right revealed them to be walking down the central aisle, reassuring passengers as they went. I glowered at how the Captain's warning didn't seem to apply to them.

I looked over a woman's curly head to get a look through the nearest window. I looked just long enough to see the storm still raging outside. Another raw lightning bolt tore its way through the dark clouds in the distance. The queasy feeling in my stomach made me start walking back to my seat. I just hoped those damned stewardesses left me alone between here and there.

I barely started walking before lightning flashed again on the right. This one was so close, all the passengers sitting next to it had to shield their eyes with raised hands. While they gave their gasps of surprise and moans of discomfort, the sound of an explosion reverberated through the cabin. Thunder.

Our plane shook again as if it'd just hit a speed bump. I reached for the nearest seat to steady myself while the passengers only grew louder. *This is insane*, I thought. *Light-*

ning never strikes the same place twice. Or was that just some old wives' tale?

The overhead lights blinked once, twice before going out. The plane lurched to its right side, scaring me enough to turn on my heel and start making a beeline for one of the vacant jump seats in the back. To hell with getting back to my proper seat. The time to comply with the Captain's orders was now, by whatever means necessary.

Some of the passengers were starting to scream. I could just hear the stewardesses over them, trying to calm them back down. *Yeah, fat chance there*, I thought while we staggered to the left. *A hundred people strapped to a flying hunk of metal fighting its way through a thunderstorm twenty thousand feet in the sky...what did they expect?* This floating tin can had just become Panic Central. Until the Captain found us some clear sky, that's how it was going to stay.

But we'd be fine, I knew. I'd been on enough planes to know getting hit by lightning wasn't *that* rare an occurrence. Stick a big fat metal tube into a bank of stormy clouds and it was bound to happen once in a while. That's why planes were designed to withstand such. I'd read once that a metal framework was built around them to conduct any stray current to the tail. That way, jolts like what we'd been hit with wouldn't damage the aircraft.

The emergency lighting flickered on, bathing the cabin in a faint yellowish hue. It added an ominous look to the scene, making the travellers' pale, frightened faces even paler. The elements outside weren't relenting one bit. Lightning kept flashing again and again as we ploughed onward through the storm clouds.

I entered the back galley, zeroing in on the nearest jump seat. I pushed it down and sat. As I reached for the safety belt, we dipped to the side again, making it harder for me to find it. Emergency lighting was poor back here and my fingers struggled to make sense of the straps. It took me a second to realise these seats were equipped with four-point harnesses rather than lap belts. That made sense, given how you have to take more precautions in the event of an emergency.

I had the two left straps snapped into the central buckle when a violent shake rattled my teeth. The plane's sudden drop left my bum floating inches above the seat and a third lightning strike mingled with the passengers' rollercoaster screams. The jolt of the impact tossed me into the *lavvy*, flat on my stomach. Pain exploded behind my temples, blood oozing between my fingers. Before I could identify what object had caused this, the plane dipped forward, making my stomach leap into my throat.

Even though my arms trembled in harmony with the plane, I managed to push myself to my knees. I wondered if the captain was attempting a landing manoeuvre. Had we reached Kiruna yet? If so, why no announcement? Was he just too busy keeping us steady? I tried to stave off the implications of those answers while listening for the familiar sound of landing gear lowering under my feet—which never came.

I pressed a palm against the *lavvy*'s walls to pull myself up. I had managed to get one foot under me when another sideways lurch reacquainted me with the light-blue partition. Seconds before I faceplanted like a starfish, a strong hand caught my coat collar, stopping my nose inches from being pulverised.

The hand yanked me to my feet and pushed me to the back of the plane. Amid the screams, my insistent rescuer was shouting something at me while half-dragging me back to the jump seats. I looked over my shoulder to catch the words. I saw a young, curly-haired woman latched to my collar. No matter how much I strained, there was no understanding her. The turbulence and rumbling were just too loud.

Her next words became a scream as the moan of torn metal accompanied a booming blow to the craft that sent us both flying into the jump seats. Now we were officially crashing. It sounded like a wing had been torn off.

Neither I nor the girl wasted time unfolding the seats and strapping ourselves in. I had just buckled the last strap when the emergency lights went out altogether.

Our plane had been turned into a floating washing machine program. My screams mingled with the rest as we shook, spun and rolled erratically. In the dim light, I saw the silhouette of passengers flying out of their seats, hitting the ceiling, becoming the targets of loose luggage.

The plane hit something right before deep yawns of protesting metal drowned out everything else. The seat's straps dug deep into my flesh while they tried keeping me in place on this rollercoaster ride to hell.

As we were thrown left and right, the acrid smell of smoke and burned wires engulfed us. I fought not to pass out, but it was a losing battle from the start. My last conscious thought was how something had to be seriously wrong for me to feel fresh air and rain hitting me in the face.

3

BLOOD AND RAIN

ANNE-MARIE - 01 AUGUST

Everything hurt.

Everything, everywhere hurt.

I barely had the strength to moan about it. Even moaning hurt. The simple act of thinking—that hurt too. My entire body ached, its youthfulness absent. I felt as if I'd been turned into a grandmother overnight.

It took time for things to start to make sense, time for me to remember I had limbs and could move them. When I tried to move them, I instantly regretted it. A hot flash of pain tore through my left leg, ripping a scream out of me. I scrunched my eyes closed harder, made myself take a few deep breaths. In...out...in...out...

I had no idea where I was. Outdoors was a dead certainty, but that was as far as I got. The air was crisp and cold, smelling of earthy moss. Twigs cracked underneath me as I attempted to unfold. Careful not to move my leg again, I pushed myself up on my forearms and blinked my eyes open, peering through a curtain of long brown hair and the odd blade of grass.

Above me, a pale midday sun was trying hard to shine through low-hanging clouds. I looked down to the sight of rain-covered green moss. It felt cold and wet on my hands. A little more to the right, there was a triangular piece of metal. All three edges looked sharp, like it was torn free of something larger. It had little brothers and sisters protruding from the moss here and there, all around me. The little silvery debris caught and reflected the sunlight at odd angles. There was stone debris as well, little and not-so-little pieces of rock that had been torn free, as though they'd been caught in an explosion. Like the surrounding moss, they were covered in rain. As a shiver ran through me, reverberating in every single one of my vertebrae, I realised I was too. What had happened? Where was I?

I pushed myself harder off the muddy ground. Twisting my hips just the right way, I got myself into a sitting position. My pelvis felt sore and I stayed mindful of my injured leg. If the pain was any indication of the extent of the injury, then my leg was torn up something fierce. But I hadn't glanced at it yet; I was afraid to. Pushing back the unavoidable, I kept looking at my surroundings instead.

This clearing didn't look familiar; I was certain I'd never been here before. I saw more debris and a few sparse birch trees in the distance. It was a tree line demarcating the edge of a wooded area. Behind me, stones and boulders dotted the landscape, culminating in a large rock formation that hid the horizon. As mountain ranges went, it was a small one, the type that was so ragged with sharp edges that it was impossible to climb. Moss covered its base while the rest of the stone had been eaten away by time and wind. The only exception was the very top, showing some recent clean, crisp cuts.

The glint of something metallic in the distance caught my eye. Whatever it was, it was trapped in a fresh-looking fissure. The sight of that kicked my brain into gear. Something big had crashed into that mountain top recently. But what? It took me longer than it should have to come up with the answer. My head felt cottony, too heavy. My poor brain felt as sore and unaccustomed to whatever was happening as the rest of me. I had just come to the conclusion that I had a concussion—God it hurt when the thoughts came rushing back in—when the answer finally came. I'd been on a plane, hadn't I? I wasn't any more—because we'd crashed.

Memories collided with each other at that realisation. The blue and yellow interior of the cabin, the rain beating down on the windows. The multiple lightning strikes, the cabin lights going out. The turbulence so violent it'd thrown an elderly man to the floor next to me. The fear that gripped me as the plane started to shake and lean on the right side. The impulse to help that I hadn't been able to fight when I saw that fellow passenger not able to get back to his feet on his own.

I know that I'd helped him make it to the crew seats in the back. But then what?

"Think, Anne-Marie, think," I muttered to myself. But nothing came. The tape in my head had no more footage to share.

Even though my mind was drawing a blank, it wasn't hard to guess what had followed. I'd been on a plane. I wasn't anymore. The plane had crashed. It was never getting back up. End of story. As my mum would say, there was no sense looking for noon when it was 2 pm.

Right now, I was alone and out in the open. I needed to get moving, find some shelter from the rain, maybe some help. The plane and the other passengers, they couldn't be that far from me. I had to get up and find them. Judging by the way my body felt, that was not going to be an easy task. In fact, it felt like it was going to be one of the hardest things I'd ever done.

When I looked down at my injured leg, the source of my discomfort was obvious. There was a large gash on my thigh, about twenty centimetres long. All around the tear, my blue jeans were soaked in blood. The wound was raw and seemed to flare as my gaze settled on it.

I took off my sweater and fastened it around the wound, binding it as tightly as I could. I had a T-shirt underneath, the cold air on my bare forearms a welcome distraction from the pain.

With nothing to grab onto as leverage, I screamed as I got to my feet. I was forced to put pressure on both legs to steady myself. When the left one protested the action, I screamed again.

Both screams were met with silence. I knew what that meant. Help was nowhere nearby. If I wanted to find any on my own, I had to get a move on. Simplifying things was the fact there weren't a lot of directions to choose from. The mountain curving inward at my back was a dead end, leaving only the birch forest ahead. About a kilometre away, I could see a plume of smoke rising from beneath the treetops, just a little to my left. I decided to aim for it. With my leg, it'd be an arduous journey, but well worth it if someone—or, better yet, painkillers—was waiting at the finish line. I started walking, one step at a time, favouring my injured leg as much as I could.

Past the first row of trees, I found a broken branch to use as a staff. It was thick enough to take all my weight, but not too heavy to carry around. Sun-dappled leaves created flickering shadows on the ground while I marched through clumps of moss, mindful of hidden tree roots. Five minutes later, I'd broken into a sweat and my breath came in short puffs. Though my exhaustion grew, I had no choice but to keep moving.

The only sounds I heard were the wind rustling through the leaves and the spongy crunch of layers under my feet. With no path in sight, I made my own. It wasn't such an arduous feat; the trees here grew further apart than I was used to seeing. They were also smaller in girth, a bit like the strong oak trees that grew high on mountainsides back home, near snow level. It made me wonder how far north of the map we were.

My brain felt sluggish as I tried to remember what one of the attendants had said. Thirty minutes away from...Kiruna, I think it was. But that was by airplane standards. I had no idea what that converted to in kilometres, or even if we'd been on course when we went down. Besides, it wasn't as if my battered brain could do the maths. But I could keep moving, so I did.

The sweet scent of the musty moss was soon replaced by the acrid smell of smoke. It grew thicker the closer I got to its source, more and more debris littering the surrounding ground. I quickened my pace as much as my throbbing leg would let me, determined to reach the fire's origin.

It turned out to be the tail section of the plane; or rather, what was left of it. It lay on its side, its left elevator fin crushed beneath the gaping broken tube of metal. Large plumes of black smoke billowed out from the tip. What remained of the plane seemed to have been torn free near the last row of seats, wires and hydraulic lines spilling out from the poor machine's ruptured skin. Remembering that I was in there not so long ago, I was surprised that I'd survived that level of devastation, let alone being thrown so far.

The front of the plane, the pilots' cabin, the rows of seats where dozens of passengers had sat, the massive wings...all of that was missing. It was as if an angry giant had torn the plane in two during a tantrum, then dropped the rear here and thrown the rest away, somewhere well out of sight.

No matter how much I looked about, I couldn't see anything more than debris-covered moss and a wounded forest. Two birch trees had fallen, with a third leaning dangerously against one of its brothers. No sign of the front of the plane... had it kept flying without its rear? Was it possible for an airplane to do that without its tail? I didn't know. As long as it had both its wings, maybe it could glide for a little while.

The reality of what I was seeing started to sink in. The full weight of it knocked the wind out of me, making me glad for the dead branch I had to lean on. Tears started rolling down my cheeks and I couldn't decide if it was from the smoke or the thought of what had happened to the other passengers. Either way, my eyes stung like that day my cousin found a pepper spray bottle and decided to have some 'fun' with me.

The depth of what I was looking at would not let up. There was nothing else here, only the broken, fuming tail-end of a plane and me. There was no rescue team coming, no helpful bystanders. I was alone with the plane wreckage—it was alone with me.

To counter the despair, my brain was quick to come up with reassuring thoughts. Maybe we were in a remote area. Maybe the nearest road was a few kilometres away and the rescue teams had to hike to get here. Maybe they were busy tending to the rest of the passengers. *Yes, of course, that had to be it,* I thought. *It's natural for these things to take time. When a huge plane falls out of the sky, burning on fire, someone's bound to see it. They had to. Otherwise...did it even happen?*

Everything was going to be fine. I just had to be patient and give them some time to find me. I was overreacting, overthinking it like I always do. I just had to wait it out until people came and found me. That was what happened when planes crashed. Everything was going to be alright...just fine.

My battered leg begged me to sit down, cutting off my happy chatter. I could feel the rest of my body's will to crumple in on itself and curl into a tight ball. There was a broken tree nearby with a sturdy trunk that looked damn inviting, but I fought the urge, tempting as it was. I knew that if I sat down, I'd never find the strength to stand back up again.

While I was thinking, cold droplets of rain started falling at irregular intervals. My T-shirt was now drenched and I was freezing. I had to find a way to warm up and to escape these angry skies. Once again, there weren't many options to choose from. I was a sitting duck...a sitting, frozen duck.

Though smoke billowed from the tail's tip, the rest of it looked safe enough for the moment. Leaning hard on my makeshift cane, I ambled closer to it. Even though it was a short walk, the razor-sharp debris embedded in the ground made it difficult to navigate. Slurping sounds punctuated each of my steps, getting worse the closer I got to the wreckage. The ground around the crash site was imbibed in more liquid than the light rain could explain. Something must have leaked out of the tail-end. Was one of the fuel tanks damaged from the crash? I didn't think they were located at the back of the plane, but then, I didn't know much about planes. Fearing that the liquid might be fuel, I stopped and bent as low as my leg allowed to press my fingers to the ground. Bringing it back to my nose, I inhaled the scent. The fluid had no particular smell, and petrol is distinctive, easy to recognise. I carried on, my sneakers sinking a little more with each fresh step.

By the time I reached the tail, I was breathing hard. What was left of the metal tube I'd flown on was resting at an odd angle, the gaping opening about fifty centimetres from the ground. Getting in there without further damaging my leg was going to be easier said than done. In the end, I decided to turn my back to the opening, sit on the ridge, and then swing my legs inside, being careful not to tear the backs of my legs on the torn carbon fibre and metal edging the wreck. I didn't know if the wires hanging from the side of the plane were live, so I was also careful not to touch them.

The torn-up blue carpet near the entrance was water-logged but the back of the plane looked to have been spared the elements. Despite a little smoke inside, the air remained breathable. And aside from the odd angle it was resting at, the tail-end seemed safe to navigate.

With the carcass tilted in this manner, I had to walk on the walls more than on the floor, dodging the remains of the awkwardly protruding last row of seats. I had to force myself to forget that three people had been sitting there the last time I saw this spot.

Having left my makeshift cane outside, I used my surroundings to help me stay upright. The crash had torn the left-hand-side loo door right off its hinges, the door itself now nowhere in sight. Mindful not to fall into the cubicle, I stepped over the opening, peering inside to make sure it was empty. Once I was across, I reached forward and opened the door to the restroom facing me. Gravity swung it open with more force than I expected. I barely had time to duck to avoid being slapped in the face.

Shards of mirror washed down from the opening of that tiny cubicle like glittering rain. It wasn't the only thing to escape. Dark brown water came down alongside the shards, the smell accompanying it leaving little doubt as to its substance. The impulse to puke was hard to rein in, so I exhaled vehemently, doing my best to cover my nostrils with my arm.

Once I was sure my stomach had settled back down, I glanced into the loo. Everything inside was broken beyond recognition. I doubted anyone could have survived the crash while being stuck in that tiny space. After thanking the heavens that no-one had been in there, I continued my journey toward the back of the plane.

Hoping to find a med-kit, I moved to the space behind the loos. I knew the crew had kept some of their equipment there. What I actually found, strapped into one of the crew's seats, was the last thing I expected.

4

TWENTY STEPS

ANNE-MARIE - 01 AUGUST

The jump seat where I'd been sitting was nothing but a memory. Half the harness was missing and the seat itself had been torn beyond recognition, which explained why I woke where I did. In the other jump seat, closer to the bulkhead, sat the man I'd helped earlier. Both of his feet dangled in the air at an awkward angle, his torso held in place by the blue harness. Passed out like this, he resembled a giant rag doll or one of those flimsy crash test dummies.

I didn't have a good look at him earlier; in the confusion, I'd only caught the briefest flash of his face under a layer of silvery hair. Now that I could see him without the world coming to an end around us, I noticed that he looked older than I'd first thought. To say nothing of a lot frailer; his business suit did little to hide how thin he was underneath it.

I called out to him, but his eyes remained closed, his limbs immobile. As I leaned closer, I noticed a trail of dried blood on his right temple. It ran from the root of his silver hair to his clean-shaven jaw. My breath caught in my throat at the sight.

Was he...? Was he—

I couldn't bring myself to finish the thought, especially since he was the only person I'd found. I needed him to be alive.

I shook myself and climbed up to him, minding the treacherous terrain. I'd had to learn first-aid when I applied for a driving licence, but now that I needed it, I couldn't remember a single thing I'd learned in class.

Assessing the wounds was a thing, wasn't it? I thought, racking my brains. *Not moving the injured person was another...or was I supposed to move him to the recovery position?* For the life of me—or him—I couldn't remember which was best.

I reached for the man's throat with my fingertips, taking in his face as I did. Even the freckles on his cheeks looked ashen. His thin, pale lips were parted, but I couldn't tell if any air was passing through them. I pressed my fingers to his throat, not daring to apply too much pressure. His skin was cold to the touch, but I had no way of knowing if that was because of the weather or the alternative. Even though I didn't feel a pulse, I wasn't sure if I was doing it right; I'd never taken anyone's pulse before. I kept moving my fingers about, but every inch of the skin I touched felt the same.

A soft moan made me jerk my fingers away and recoil in surprise. My eyes locked onto his face in time to see his eyes shift underneath his closed lids. The first lines of a furrowed brow started to form above his thick, bushy eyebrows. Well...that was as good a sign of life as any. Thank heaven I wasn't alone anymore.

I called out to him again, reaching out to rub his arm. Try though I did to coax him back to consciousness, he remained out of it. Scrunching up my own brow, I fought to remember more of those first-aid classes. All that did was make my thoughts a contradictory mess. I kept going back to one contradiction in particular. On one hand, our instructor had warned us that moving an injured person was dangerous and should be avoided; there was no telling what internal injuries the victim could be suffering from, so any kind of movement could worsen an injured spine or even kill. But at the same time, I could also remember lectures on the benefits of the recovery position and how manhandling unconscious people into it would ensure they could breathe more easily. So which would work here?

Biting at my lower lip in puerile anxiety, I looked at the man more closely. The sole visible injury was the head wound I'd caught earlier. Other than that, and the fact he was out of it, he seemed fine.

What decided it for me was how uncomfortable the poor man looked. With the way the tail-end of the plane was positioned, he was dangling on his left side with his left leg thrown over his right. The left shoulder strap was doing most of the work of keeping him in his seat, but it was also cutting hard into the skin of his neck. Another hour of that and the belt would draw blood. I moved closer so that he would lean on me rather than fall to the floor. Then I reached for the buckle.

This stranger may have been thin, but he wasn't lightweight. Taking most of his weight on me was like getting stabbed in the leg all over again. My back complained and wounds I hadn't been aware of before flared up in protest. I forced all of that pain to the back of my mind, focusing on the task at hand. I had to get him out of here and to safety.

My human load remained limp the whole way, not once

waking up. If it weren't for the occasional moan of pain, I'd have thought I was carrying a store manikin.

I left him lying on the cabin floor as I got off the plane. I took a moment to make sure my left leg was steady under my feet. Then, reaching under his shoulders, I dragged him outside. I tried cradling his head and neck as much as possible, praying that I wasn't doing more harm than good.

I dragged him away from the wreckage, his shiny leather shoes leaving deep grooves in the wet soil behind us, trying hard to keep him from soaking up too much of the fluid on the ground. A part of me kept worrying that what was left of the plane could blow up or something. I had no idea how far away we had to get to be safe if that happened. My battered body managed twenty steps before my leg gave out under me and I fell to the ground. I dragged my fellow passenger down with me, though I tried to cushion his fall by landing in a heap underneath him. This would have to be far enough from the plane.

Since he wasn't protesting the change in altitude, I stayed there for a few long minutes. I focused on my breathing while I also fought not to lose consciousness again. When the pain in my leg was too much, I pushed myself free of the man's bulk and lay beside him.

Noticing my sweater had come loose during the tumble, I fastened it back in place around my thigh with clenched teeth. More deep breaths followed as I collapsed back into the soil. As I lay there, gasping and wheezing, I was flabbergasted at how eerily quiet the surrounding forest was. It dawned on me that I hadn't seen or heard any kind of animals since I'd woken up. I hadn't seen a bird taking flight, never mind the bark of a rescue dog. Everything around us felt like a silent graveyard; the final resting place of a metallic bird that had never made it home.

Dark, black smoke continued to escape from the tip of the tail. As big a contrast as it was from our surroundings, there was little doubt it could be seen from a good distance. The foliage encasing us wasn't that thick, so it shouldn't have been too hard to pinpoint our location. Were my fellow passenger and I so far removed from any roads that rescuers had to hike to get to us? Surely they had helicopters that could get to us faster. So why weren't they already circling our position?

The man next to me broke off my thought by moaning, making me turn back to him. His face wasn't as lax as it'd been on the plane. Lines of pain were etched at the corners of his eyes and mouth that not even the deepest of wrinkle could hide. Was I responsible for that?

Now that I could see him in plain light, I realised he wasn't as old as I'd thought. I've never been good at guessing people's ages but I'd put him at somewhere around sixty. He had the right suit and sleek haircut to be a businessman. A nice look but not a practical one under the circumstances. Not that I had much room to talk, seeing as I was so cold in my T-shirt and jeans. Still, it had to be bad for him too. The fact he had so little meat on his bones also didn't help.

While dragging him all the way here may have saved him from smoke inhalation and possibly an explosion, no one would congratulate me if he died from hypothermia as a result. Not that I was expecting any form of congratulations in the first place, but still...

I remembered seeing a blanket on the floor next to the jump seats. I tilted my head back and sighed. The only way I was going to get it was by going back in. My leg was in such bad shape, the throbbing near constant now, that I wasn't sure if I could stand on it again, much less walk. But one look at the silent forest around us and at the wounded man lying unconscious next to me sealed the deal. Wounded or not, I was the only one who could do the job. Not counting on others to do your job was something my family had pushed onto me from an early age. Who knew it would come in handy at a time like this?

Planting both my palms down and forcing my good leg to fold beneath me, I pushed myself upright with a scream. Tears of pain ran down my cheeks as I ambled forward, one shaky step at a time. Twenty steps, twenty little steps. That was all the walking I needed to do...So close and yet so far away.

I was panting, sweating and shivering by the time I finished heaving myself back inside the metallic tube. I moved past the loos to aim straight for the rear galley. Wasn't that also where the staff kept their food and the rest of their stuff? I could have done with a warm coffee and a sandwich right then. And a heavy dose of painkillers.

After I found the blanket I'd seen earlier, I kept looking for more. While there was nothing useful near the folding-seats, the other side of the plane had a dozen light grey storage containers affixed to the back wall, secured with red safety latches. This had to be where the crew had stored some of the equipment. I was thankful that nothing on them had moved during the turbulences and subsequent crash. Unlike, well...everything else.

Since I had no idea what was stored where, I just opened the first container I could reach. Inside, I found a stock of drinks, two dozen plastic cups, a pile of blue and yellow kid's toys, a pretty full trash bin and some of the food-boxes we'd been served on the flight. Since the latter were unopened, I dug right into the food, ready to wolf down anything I could get my hands on.

Today's lunch had been a small portion of too-dry salmon with a weird-looking dill sauce and two baked potatoes. It tasted as bad as it had in the air, but I didn't mind half as much now. I needed all the energy I could get.

In the next container, I found spare blankets, blue with a couple of yellow lines in the corner. I took a couple out, placing them in a pile next to a bottle of water I'd taken out of the first locker. Since I had nothing to carry everything in, I unfolded one of the blankets and bundled everything into it. That accomplished, I tied the corners together into a makeshift sack. While it was heavy, the vital contents inside made it well worth the weight. I hauled my treasure trove back behind me.

The way out was just as excruciating as the way in, if not more so. Those last twenty steps from wrecked plane to unconscious passenger used what little energy the food had given me. I crumbled next to my insensate companion, laying down on my back and becoming a puddle of aching limbs. My arms and legs throbbed as they began to calm themselves down, my breathing slowing down as well. My body was sending me so many conflicting signals, I couldn't make sense of them all. Pain, cold, fatigue, warmth, sweating...If there was one word that would sum them up it would be "Enough!" I so needed to rest. I couldn't remember a time that I'd ever felt this weak.

In the quiet of the deserted forest, I could still hear the man's ragged breathing, a sure sign that he was alive. Nothing else disturbed the quiet. The daylight had lessened in the last hour, telling me that dusk wasn't too far away.

Neither of us were ready for the night chill. My companion needed help and once again, there was no one else to provide it but me. Taking in a deep breath through my nose, I dug into my last reserves of strength to sit back up.

Upon closer inspection, I could see the man was shivering with each exhale. One of his hands had moved up, cradling his middle. Pressing the water bottle to his lips, I managed to make him swallow a few gulps, which was a relief in itself. Next, I reached for the bag of blankets with a grunt of pain before untying the bundle. I used the three blankets inside it to cover him up, saving the last one for myself.

I lay back down on the soft wet ground, totally spent. I'd done all I could for today. As I sunk back into oblivion, I hoped the blankets would be enough to keep him—and me—alive until help got here.

5

FIRST IMPRESSIONS

KILLIAN - 02 AUGUST

The cold woke me up. Or was it the *chitter*? I'd been vibrating all night like a rogue smartphone. Did I leave a window open?

Dampness on my back registered about a second later. And then the pain. A splitting headache that made me wonder how much I'd had to drink the night before.

I groaned as I sat up, pushing the blankets aside. I wondered why the smell of smoke was so tight in my bedroom; I'd always hated the smell of fags. I never let anyone partake of that nasty habit in my room, no matter how much liquor I'd imbibed.

My fingers curled around a rougher blanket than I antici-pated. My fingers came away wet. *The hell?* I thought, the first clear thought that punched through my brain fog.

I forced my eyes open, settling on a green canopy that allowed what seemed to be late-afternoon sunlight to shine through. I was glad that the sun had begun to set. I didn't think I could have handled the harsh spikes of a full-blown ball of light. This hangover was just too much.

As I let my gaze fall, my eye settled on a great smashed tube of metal. It seemed familiar somehow. That's when a flood of memories opened up, making my headache worse. My run through the airport in Geneva. The plane repeatedly hit by lightning in mid-flight. The harrowing descent towards the bottom in the dark. It all came back to me in a rush.

I groaned, realising that yes, this day could get worse after all. For there it lay, the broken tail-end section of the plane I'd been on. Cabin torn and gaping near the back, resting at an odd angle amidst the foliage and rain-soaked dirt. It hadn't been a dream. The nightmare I'd had was as real as the wreckage I saw before me.

It hurt to stand back up, and a wave of nausea hit me when I got back to my feet. I waited it out before taking a couple of shaky steps towards the mess of metal and plastic that used to be my flight to Sweden. Where was the other end of it? Or the other passengers? Or the rescue?

I looked about, working my way around the broken tail, but finding nothing except sparse trees and more debris. It didn't make any sense. Someone else had to be here. I didn't remember making it out of the plane and lying down. Or getting the blankets.

"*Hullo?*" I called out, loud as I could. It ended in a cough, making me realise my throat was sore and parched. I swallowed and tried again with, "Is anybody here?" More coughing. This time, it continued until it became full-on hacking.

After clearing my throat, I allowed it to settle. That's when I realised that I had no idea where 'here' was. It looked like a forest, but not a very dense one. It was dreary and misty, like a location for a 70s slasher horror film. The trees weren't that thick or high, growing further apart than what I was used to seeing in central Europe. If memory served, that only happened when trees were planted in high altitude or very far north on the map. Since oxygen levels seemed normal, Option Two had to be what explained the scrawny vegetation.

I finished my circle of the tail but found no clue that would help me figure out my location. A glance down at my wristwatch left me with yet more questions. According to the timepiece, it was close to two in the morning. Given how much I'd paid for it, I was inclined to trust it. But then, luxury didn't always mean durability, did it? On top of that, my eyes were telling me a different story. The sun was out, bathing the surrounding forest in what amounted to early morning or late-evening light.

The midnight sun, as it was called, only happened around the summer solstice and in places north of the Arctic Circle or south of the Antarctic Circle. And Stockholm, our plane's initial destination, was hundreds of miles south of the Arctic Circle. Another proof, as if I needed one, that we'd crashed way off-course. *What of Kiruna*, I wondered. *Was it that far north?*

Looking down at my wristwatch brought more bad news. The plane had crashed about ten hours ago. Ten whole, long hours was more than enough time for several rescue teams to have been mobilised. So where were they?

The Swedes—if this was Sweden—weren't known to be slackers. They ought to have been able to track the plane's signal by now using the radar information, or to use satellites to find the plane's black boxes—which, I realised, could be hundreds of miles away, if they were in the front half of the plane. With its tall white and blue tail, what was left of the plane stood out like a sore thumb amongst the green foliage here, so if there were people nearby, they should have seen it. Even on the grainiest of satellite footage, only a blind idiot could miss it, or the large gouge the thing had made into the soft earth.

A feeble moan came from my left, and I froze. Turning on my side, I saw the soggy heap of blankets I'd woken up under move and rustle, like there was someone—or something—there. I held my breath as it squirmed out from under the blue and yellow mass of linen.

Some of my questions were answered when a mop of curly brown hair emerged from beneath the rough material. It was followed up by the round sleepy face of a young woman. After giving thanks to the universe that she wasn't some wild creature who'd come to see what was happening, I gave her a closer look.

She had white but tanned skin, looking to be twenty-something. Half of her hair was matted to the side of her face. The rest of it was a mess of wild curls that only the sturdiest of combs could tame. Though she was blinking her blue eyes open, she hadn't spotted me yet. When her gaze finally settled on me, she seemed as surprised to see me as I was to see her.

She recovered quickly, bringing up a hand to vainly try to rearrange her hair while sitting up. All her fingers did was get trapped in the tangled mess, so she just scratched at her scalp instead.

She made motions like she was going to get to her feet. Then she stopped, seeming to think it wasn't such a good idea. So instead, she pushed the blankets off her. When the flesh of her bare arms met the cold morning air, she shivered.

It was only when the last blanket came off that I finally

understood her reluctance about standing up. She'd used what looked like a sweater to bandage up her left leg. Despite the makeshift tourniquet, there were trails of caked blood going all the way to her ankle.

I moved closer to her. I had a million questions, but the first one that made it past my lips was the immediate one. "*Oi*, do you know how I got off the plane?"

She looked at me like I'd grown an extra head. I figured it might have been the Scottish accent. When our brogue gets thick enough, only we Scots can understand it. So I tried to dial it down with my next question. "Was that you who pulled me out of there?"

No answer. But it must have been her. I sure as hell didn't see any other volunteers. Just my luck that I'd get someone who didn't understand English. I took a deep breath before pointing at the broken tail. "Plane." Then I pointed at myself. "Me." Lastly, my finger landed on the crumpled pile of soggy blue and yellow blankets. "There."

That little pantomime got me a positive nod. I wasn't sure how to feel about that. This woman was little more than a teenager. And she didn't seem too bright at that. I mean, who in Europe doesn't know a little English these days?

I reached for my handkerchief. While I rummaged through my pocket, I checked to make sure my wallet was still there. Sure, this girl had been able to afford a plane ticket, but everything about her, her faded jeans, worn-out trainers and flowery T-shirt, screamed middle-class. Nothing they won't do to nab an extra euro.

I was careful to hide my relief when my fingertips came in contact with my leather-bound wallet. I had half a mind to pull it out—along with the handkerchief, of course—just to check its content. But if she was a thief and knew I was onto her, it was anyone's guess how she'd react. Since I had nothing to defend myself with and there wasn't anyone else around to help, I decided to err on the side of caution.

"Where's everyone?" I asked. "Where's the rescue?"

I got that same fish-out-of-the-water expression out of her. I wondered what I'd done to deserve being stuck with such a simpleton. "Rescue," I enunciated slowly, then swiping my hand about in a circle, "Where?"

She shook her head before looking around herself. It was as if she was searching for something, which she seemed to find a minute later. Without standing up, she scrambled closer to the wreckage until she reached a broken tree branch. *What did she intend to do with that?* I thought, feeling a pang of fear that I hated admitting to.

I got up and took a step back as her fingers curled around it before she brought it closer to her torso. She paused and glanced up at me. Surprise stretched the tired lines of her face for just an instant before going away.

She turned her head back to the branch, placed it in a vertical position and then used it to haul herself up onto her feet. She did that with a groan of pain, panting hard by the time she was upright again. She tested her damaged leg by applying pressure on her foot for a few seconds. A pain-filled cry later, she gave up and returned to leaning on the makeshift cane.

From under that curtain of mad curls, she glanced at me again. Seemingly satisfied that I hadn't moved, she started walking, one careful step at a time. I had to admit that she used the cane well through her limping, never once giving in to the weakness in her bad leg.

While she wasn't far from the gaping entrance to the plane, it was obviously taking a lot for her to get there. But she completed her hike and hoisted herself inside the wreckage, ever mindful of the sharp metallic shards near the tube's mouth. Then she disappeared into the shadows.

"What are you doing?" I called after her. When I got no response, I carefully walked towards the plane myself. *Maybe it wasn't that she didn't understand English?* I thought. *Maybe she's just deaf? Or simply rude?*

I got close enough to see the tail had been torn off somewhere between the last row of seats and the twin lavatories. A weak spot in the plane's frame—a section junction, if I had to guess. The cobalt blue carpet was in shreds near the gap, both plastic and metal showing signs of having been torn off. But I looked about at the trees and what lay beyond without seeing any sign of the other half. Save for a few dark clouds, the skies were clear. Everything around us was calm and quiet. It'd been this way since I woke up and I didn't like it one bit. What kind of things could be—

Clang!

The sound interrupted my thoughts, making me glance inside the wrecked plane. "What the hell are you even doing in there, *lassie?*" I asked, leaning closer to the opening. Near as I could tell in the gloom, she'd disappeared somewhere in the back and was now tinkering with...something. It sounded like she was opening and closing containers. "*Oi!* You could answer me, you know. Are you going to make me come after you?"

The only answer I got was more banging and clanging. I decided the way she'd gotten in the plane was probably the safest. I turned my back to the opening, sat on the edge and while turning onto myself, brought both my legs inside. Once I was back on my feet, I moved to the back of the tail. Thankfully, what was left of the plane was sturdy, albeit difficult to navigate. The floor was at a diagonal angle, which didn't make crossing through it any easier with my entire body still sore from the crash.

I found the girl busy opening and closing doors and drawers in the galley. The little hussy was raiding it, which made me worry about my wallet again. While she had her back turned to me, I moved my wallet from my trouser pocket to the inside breast pocket of my coat. *Try getting your hands on it now, you little thief,* I thought, mentally snickering in satisfaction while giving her a condescending glare.

My fellow passenger, having found a large bin bag, started tossing items into it, left and right. Water bottles, candy bars, blankets...everything went. She didn't seem to mind that I was witnessing her crime, and carried on as though I wasn't there. *Who did this bloody millennial think she was?* I thought with a sneer. Entitlement...that was the problem with this generation. They acted as if they'd already inherited the earth.

"They're not going to let you keep that, you know," I said, leaning back against the side of the upturned *cludgie.* "You're going to have to return every bit of it when help gets here."

My words didn't affect her, didn't stop her from reaching into the last compartment. By then, her bin bag was almost full. I wondered how she envisioned her getaway. She was a tall one, granted...maybe five-eight or five-nine, nearly my height. But that damn bag was as tall as her hips and was heavy to boot. I could tell the heft when she strained to pull the bag after her.

"And now what?" I asked, unable to keep the mirth out of my voice, at the sheer stupidity of all she was doing. "However are you going to get it out now, *lassie?*"

She tried taking a step forward and winced. I realised

she'd abandoned her makeshift cane, had been doing all her looting hopping round on one foot. But there was no way she could drag her prize out without using both legs. She took another step and then a third before finally giving up. She looked up at me with unshed tears in her eyes. She didn't need words to get the message across. She wanted me to help her, though? Yeah, that was a laugh.

"*Naw*," I said, raising both hands. "Not in a million years."

She frowned at me before giving me that surprised expression again. She opened her mouth as if to say something before closing it again. She dragged the bag whatever little distance she'd made, and then some. She motioned at my hand, and then at the one of hers which was holding onto the top of the bag.

"I'm not helping you," I said as emphatically as I could. "I work for a bank, not for a thief-for-hire. You want to steal things, do it yourself, you thieving *slag!*" *What the hell was I even doing in here?* I wondered. If this punk wanted to commit a felony, I was better off away from this crime scene. What if someone walked in on us right then? They'd think I was in on it and who could blame them? Ridiculous, the gall of these entitled youths.

"Yeah, I'm leaving you to it," I said. "You're on your own here."

The only reply I got from her was a grab of my hand as I turned to leave. I froze, unsure if it was out of surprise or fear. Not minding my reaction, she reached for something inside her bag. An instant later, she slapped a water bottle inside my empty palm. I left without saying another word to her...not that it'd help. I only kept the water bottle because I was parched.

6

BREAKFAST FOR TWO

KILLIAN - 02 AUGUST

I'd had time to drink half the bottle and relieve myself behind a tree when she came out of the wreck, dragging that damned plastic bin bag behind her. She struggled to get it off the gaping mouth of the cabin tube. Seating herself down first, she dragged her loot to the forest floor before jumping down herself. Her landing was awkward, but she managed to land on her uninjured leg.

She paused an instant, her trainers sinking into the mushy ground near the entrance, before fixing me with a pointy stare. Well, if she wanted me to come and help, she was in for a long wait. I turned my back to her so I could stare at the trees some more. No matter how much I tried to see what lay beyond them, the only thing my eyes found was yet more trees.

I heard her huffing and puffing behind me, the slow draw of the bag on the floor drowning out her sticky steps. Well, she was nothing if not resilient, that one.

By the time she stepped in front of me, her cheeks were flushed an angry red, a good match for her panting and sweating. The glare she sent me from those baby blue eyes was one of a kind. Her face had an odd mix of anger, contempt and disdain that seemed so out of place on her young features. I stared back at her in bewilderment. Who the hell was this wee girl to judge me? She was the one committing a crime and yet here she was behaving as if I was the one at fault. *Bollocks* to that!

She sat down near where I stood, a couple of feet shy of the pile of blankets I'd woken up under. Well, I say "sat" when "let herself crumble to the floor in an exhausted heap" was closer to the mark. It was like she sort of melted, the way an ice sculpture does on a warm sunny day.

As soon as her hands left the plastic bin, they reached for her injured leg, which she started to massage. That's when I saw that she also had a cut on her right arm, though that was little more than a scratch. Her leg was the only visible serious injury. Still, with that sweater masking the wound, I had a hard time judging how serious. If it wasn't for the blood-stains, I'd have been tempted to think she was faking it to win sympathy.

Not minding me at all, she went rummaged through her stolen loot again. She pulled out another water bottle from the bin, uncapped it and took a couple of grateful sips. Then she recapped it before placing it on the wet ground beside her. She went for another dip inside the bag, feeling inside it a little longer. This time, she pulled out a first-aid kit.

After a long sigh, she started to unfasten her sweater with a wince. When I saw what it covered, I felt bad for her. That nasty wound on her thigh was anything but faked. Something had cut into her flesh deep and wide. Now that the pressure was off, the wound started bleeding again.

I'd never liked the sight of blood, so I glanced away,

though not quickly enough. A wave of dizziness hit me, forcing me to look around for somewhere to sit and rest myself.

I found a grand total of bugger-all. Though the rain had stopped falling, the surrounding ground was still muddy from the drops. Be damned if I was going to ruin my suit by sitting on it. Tom Ford himself would never do such a thing.

Looking at the place where I'd spent the night, I saw that it wasn't in any better condition than where I stood. Looking at that made me palm the back of my pants with a hand. I frowned at the grime my fingers found there.

I sighed and shook my head. Silly of me to think my suit wasn't ruined long before I woke up. I sat down at a reasonable distance from the makeshift surgeon next to me. She was intent on juggling her tools one-handed while trying to stem the flow of blood with a napkin. Seeing that made me think, *Oh well...a suit's something I can replace when I get back home.*

By then, the girl had a piece of jagged metal in hand, which she was using to cut away the leg of her bloody jeans. That sight made me look away again and return my attention to what was left of the plane. The smoke coming out of the tail had died down in the past few minutes. Only the tiniest of hazy tendrils remained, the dark-grey plumes going about twenty inches before they became too thin for my eyes to make out. That wasn't good news. Anyone looking for us now would have a much more difficult time of it.

Behind me, the girl was muttering something foreign under her breath. If I had to guess, she was cursing her damn fool self for making her injuries worse. I glanced at her then, saw her still working on her leg. While I was glad to discover she wasn't a mute, I was less glad to find that she definitely didn't speak English. Her words were too quiet for me to make out what language she was using. Maybe if I heard more, it'd be something I knew.

While I'd been looking at the dying smoke, she'd opened a bottle of clear liquid that smelled like iodine. Whatever it was, she poured some of it onto a cotton ball that she was using to dab into her open wound. When my stomach somersaulted, I had to look away again. *Jesus, Mary and Joseph, how the bloody hell could she stomach all that?* I thought.

As I listened to Ms Medicine Woman tend to herself, I let my gaze wander around the crash site. Seeing as there was nothing but trees, debris and the big metal tube we'd both come out of, I got bored with that in a hurry. Amidst sounds of plastic wrappers being torn open, I could hear several gasps of pain and foreign words that could only be heavy bouts of cussing and cursing. While I might have been wrong, the words sounded like French.

A while later, I cautiously turned back around. By then, the worst was over for her. She was wrapping some gauze over the wound and fastening it with a white bandage. My stomach congratulated me on finally picking the right moment to look.

By the time she was done, I realised what an odd pair we made. The two of us stranded here—wherever the hell here was—with no rescue in sight and no way to call out for help. The smoke was all but gone now and I'd left my smartphone charging next to my business class seat. Resourceful as this girl was, she didn't look like she owned a phone either. At least one she hadn't stolen first.

"Have you got a phone?" I asked. While I was almost certain what her answer would be, I had to be sure. When she gave me that confused look, I extended my thumb and pinkie to give her the universal sign language for 'talking on the phone' saying, "Telephone?" for emphasis.

She shook her head no before returning her attention to the med-kit she had in her lap.

"*Aye*," I said with a sigh. "Me neither."

After she packed up the first-aid kit, she inspected her handiwork with a critical eye. It looked like she'd done a good job with the tight white bandage around her mid-thigh, though she used way too much tape to fasten it. After she put the first-aid kit back inside the plastic bag, she pulled out two KitKats from it. She tossed me one and kept the other for herself.

The moment it landed in my lap, I realized that I was starving. I tore through it as fast as I could, not minding so much that I hadn't paid for it. As breakfast choices go, KitKats weren't anywhere near the top of my list, but after wolfing it down in under a minute, I concluded that it was the best damn KitKat I'd ever eaten.

That's when I noticed how the girl hadn't even started eating hers. She fixed me with a raised eyebrow and a smirk that spoke volumes. No translation needed to understand what it meant: "Aren't you glad I got all of this stuff now?" Christ, she was so damned smug.

I looked up through the sparse leaves at the empty skies above us. I strained my ears to capture any foreign sounds or any kind of disturbance. All I got back was the ever-present quiet that had surrounded us from the start. By the looks of things, we were going to be stuck here for a while yet.

Blame it on the crash scrambling my brains. Blame it on the stubbornness noted on my many performance reviews. But it was only at that moment when understanding finally dawned on me. This young woman hadn't been stealing at all. Despite her injuries, she'd been gathering the supplies we'd need to survive on our own out here: food, drinks, blankets, medicine.

The reason she'd shared it was because she knew we were all we had. Since help wasn't coming anytime soon, we had to stick together. She'd just been quicker on the uptake than me.

7

SOMEWHERE ON THE MAP

KILLIAN - 02 AUGUST

I woke up to the same sorry, dilapidated sight I'd fallen asleep to. The faded glory of the broken tail was still there, resting sideways in its quiet vegetation shrine. The last of the smoke had long disappeared into the grey of the not-night sky. A glance at my watch told me it was a little after six o'clock. I'd napped for only a couple of hours.

It seemed like the sun was brighter now than it'd been during the starless night. Still, it'd be another few hours until it reached full bloom. When I looked around, I realized that the woman was nowhere in sight. Given the fact she'd left the bag of supplies a few feet from me, coupled with her nasty leg wound, I doubted she'd gone far. Even so, I couldn't help but wonder where she was. Maybe she'd gone back into the plane?

Standing up, I strained my ears to hear her. The only sounds to reach them was a faint wind rustling through the trees and what sounded like waves crashing on rocks. No barks coming from search and rescue dogs, no thump-

thump of a helicopter's blades, not even the crushing of fallen tree branches under heavy boots. I didn't think I'd ever felt this alone.

The creaking of twigs behind me disturbed the silence, making me turn around to face its source. I saw the woman coming out from behind a shrub. She had her makeshift cane in hand, but seemed to be moving with a little more ease than the previous night. Cleaning the wound and applying proper bandages to it had no doubt done wonders.

Naturally, she wore the same clothes as before, but she'd since tied her curly hair into a bun, revealing more of her youthful features. Definitely mid-twenties, for sure—a baby-faced mid-twenties at that.

As her eyes settled on me, a soft smile rose to her lips. Was she glad I hadn't run away? Then again, where was there to run to?

"Have you seen anyone?" I asked. "Help?"

She paused a few feet from me and cocked her head to one side, her brows knitting. Then she shrugged her shoulders. I wasn't sure if it was because she hadn't seen anyone or if she hadn't understood the question. Probably—even likely —both, for all I knew. I doubt she'd have been alone if the answer was yes.

Hobbling back to the bag, she rummaged inside until she found another pair of KitKats. After throwing me one, we ate in silence. I couldn't shake the feeling that something was very wrong with our situation. Help should have been there by now. What, were they so busy helping the other survivors that they just assumed the tail-end of the plane was empty?

Naw, that didn't make sense. Not twenty hours after the crash. If they'd had any idea where the tail was, they'd have sent teams here by now to secure the zone. If nothing else, they'd have made sure curious civilians wouldn't come by and mess with the debris. I'd seen movies about this. The authorities had to bag and tag every last screw and bolt they could find. That way, they could later lay out all the pieces like a jigsaw, cataloguing the various wears and tears to better understand what had gone wrong. It was a slow, gruelling process, but one that always involved the first step, which was finding as much of the plane as possible, starting with the corners of the puzzle: tail, nose and both wingtips.

So, no, there had to be a good reason why they weren't here. The problem was that I couldn't find any such reason that was the least bit reassuring. It was getting harder and harder to push back on the notion that no one was coming. That this wee girl and I were truly on our own.

In any given situation, planning for the worst was a sound tactic—not one I liked to use if I could avoid it, but sound nonetheless. *So,* I reasoned to myself, *if no one is coming, I should stop wasting my time sitting around doing nothing. Right, all well and good, but what* can *I do instead?*

The starting point of getting any plan of action together was easy: knowledge. Ergo, I needed more information to fully understand this situation before moving onto the next step. Right now, the greatest unknown factor was location. *There has to be a town or a road somewhere. We just need to find it.* Even as I told myself this, doubt crept into my head telling me that I was already lousing up that first step.

I stood up and closed my eyes for a moment. Again, I could hear the faint sound of waves in the distance. I just wasn't sure which way the sound was coming from. I opened my eyes again, seeing nothing more than the ever-present trees and moss. No path in sight anywhere. Still, the vegetation wasn't dense, so it wouldn't be too hard to walk through. I just had to choose a direction to do the walking. And doing that on this little information? Ah, there was the hard part...

Behind me, I heard the woman standing up too. There was no moan of pain this time, only a heavy exhale. An instant later, she was standing by my side.

"Any idea which way to go?" I asked, waving my pointer finger around. There weren't a hundred choices to pick from. It was either forest leading to forest or forest leading to forest.

Though I was pretty certain she understood my gestures, if not my words, she remained silent and motionless. I sighed and nodded in the direction of the sun before I started walking. She managed to keep pace with me, hobbled leg and all.

After about fifteen minutes of walking through low shrubs and tree branches, the forest opened up, giving us an unobstructed view of a cliffside overlooking the sea. That vast expanse of blue welcomed us on the left and right, wild waves coming to meet us before crashing at the foot of the cliffs. The sun was a large ball of fire directly above us, rising high over the rocks that stood above the surf in certain spots like submerged fingers reaching out of the depths. The shadows those rocks cast even resembled living limbs in the way they trickled and danced on their aquatic backdrop.

I moved closer to the cliff's edge, looking around in search of something. Anything, really. But all I saw was more of the same, the edges of the cliffs curving inward until they disappeared. Not only did it seem never-ending, but it was quite a long drop to the bottom. Any fall from here would be fatal.

Finally, I spotted a small cove a little to the left, protected by a smaller set of half-submerged dark rocks set in a half-circle. When I moved closer to the edge, I could make out a little beach in those shadows, apparently made of small pebbles rather than sand. It was as croissant-shaped as the rocks themselves, about fifteen feet wide and thirty feet long.

I wondered if it was possible to get down there. While this cliff had some height, it wasn't Cornwall-high. I pegged it as forty, maybe fifty feet high at the most. And there was a chance we'd see something more from the further edges of the cove. *And* if there was a way to glimpse behind those rocks, we'd see more of the coast.

I heard the rustle of clothes behind me, turning just in time to see the woman act on the very same idea I was. She was heading down the cliff, relying on her staff more than ever. With careful steps, I went down after her. While I couldn't remember the last time I'd gone for a walk on something that wasn't concrete, she seemed to have more experience at it than I did. Despite her injury, her footing was sure, never once slipping as she forged a path between the least jagged rocks, favouring the tiny recesses where dirt had gathered. I followed as best as I could, trying to place pressure on the same surfaces she did, though that was rough on my rigid, thin ankles. I envied the woman for her ankle-high grey sneakers with their walker's treads. The soles of my dress shoes were slick, which gave me a harder time keeping my footing.

Eventually, we got to the beach at the bottom. It was as I'd pegged it, made up of an assortment of light grey pebbles the size of £2 coins. Looking back up, the looming cliff didn't look nearly as steep. The rocks provided protection from the winds and the idea of a private beach was appealing. It could even be a nice place to stay for a day, if one was looking for such a thing.

Behind me, the woman muttered something that sounded a lot like "Hell." I turned back around in surprise. Did she know some English, after all?

She was kneeling sideways by the water, bringing water-coated fingers to her lips. She shook her wet finger for emphasis before saying again, "*Sel.*" The downward twist of her lips helped with the translation. She was telling me the French word for "salt".

If this was salted water, then this couldn't be a lake or a river. That helped narrow down our location some, as it meant we weren't inland. I tried remembering the layout of Sweden, its position atop the European continent, sandwiched between Norway in the west and Finland in the east. The southern half of the country was surrounded by the Baltic Sea on all sides. The north-western part was glued to Norway, whereas the eastern stretch had the Gulf of Bothnia reaching high between Sweden and Finland. Come to think of it, wasn't the Gulf mostly made of salted water?

I shook my head and went back to the rest of my crude mental cartography. Our intended destination, Stockholm, sat next to the Baltic Sea. But after we hit the storm clouds, we'd stopped aiming to reach the capital city. Instead, we'd been re-routed to another airport that was further north. What had the stewardess said about the town the captain had mentioned—Kiruna, I think it was called? That it was hundreds of miles north of Stockholm?

Finally, I knew Sweden and Finland joined in the North, leaving no room for a body of salt water to sit. But in the west...I did some more rough calculations in my head. The Norwegian coast wasn't that far away in the west, was it?

After putting all that I knew with all I'd observed, I realised this open-horizon could only mean one of two things. We were looking at either the Norwegian Sea or the Gulf of Bothnia. While I had no way of knowing which it was, we were totally off-course either way.

8

BEARER OF BAD NEWS

KILLIAN - 02 AUGUST

Since there was nothing more for us at the cove, we headed back to the tail. I worried some about the woman's leg, but since the trek back and forth had been a short one, she seemed capable of enduring one more.

This time, I chose to go in the opposite direction, through the trees left of the gaping maw of the plane's carcass. As long as we kept the sun at our back, it'd be easy to go in a straight line. Plus, it'd also keep the sun out of our eyes, letting us move faster than if we'd been blinded by it.

I'd taken but two steps when the woman suddenly reached out to me, her fingers sneaking around my arm to stop me. I turned in surprise. She'd never come this close before, save for when she'd held me back to give me the water bottle in the plane. This time, though, her touch was calm, her manner measured and reassuring. Figuring it was important, I waited to see what she wanted.

She looked up at me, before shaking her head; the motion slow and deliberate.

"We have to try other directions, *lass*," I said. "Why not this one, eh?"

Releasing my arm, she looked like she wanted to say something before thinking better of it. With a sigh, she reached both hands up, pressing the tips of her fingers together to form a triangle.

I had no bloody idea what she meant by that. "We don't have time to play Pictionary now," I said, my displeasure easy to hear. "Make an effort to be more plain."

Huffing a breath, she pointed at the direction I'd chosen, then shook her head again, before making the triangle shape once more.

I still had no clue what she meant by that gesture. But it was obvious that she thought it was a bad idea. So why not make a cross if she didn't want us to go that way? Wasn't that the universal sign for it? Or did she not even know that much? Besides, how could she have known that it was the wrong path to follow? Had she been that way yet?

"Whatever," I muttered, pinching the bridge of my nose in frustration. "We can keep that one for last." I gestured with my pointer. "Left or right, then. The choice is yours, *lassie*."

In response, she brought both of her hands back down to her sides and took a step back. It was obvious from her confused expression that she had no idea what I'd just said.

"Just my luck isn't it." I turned left and started marching. "Stuck at the corner of 'no' and 'where' with what has to be the only passenger in the whole plane that can't understand a damned word I'm saying." Behind me, I heard the woman following. "I mean, I've spent months in Switzerland, and everyone I met there spoke some English—even if it was just a few words. Everyone!"

If the woman had any thoughts on my rant, she kept them to herself.

Less than ten minutes later, the forest cleared again and we came upon a larger beach. Aside from there being pebbles, this was nothing like the cliffs and the cove we'd seen earlier. The incline from the woods to the ocean was soft, making the beach flat. The pebbles here shared the space with light grey earthy sand, spread as far as my eye could see.

Naturally, there wasn't a soul in sight. No signs of any recent visitors either. Everything was as pristine as the rest of the land we'd walked. No markings, no litter, nothing that'd been displaced or shaped by anything other than nature. All that meant one thing: no humans.

I walked closer to the dying waves, straying from the trees to favour the newer ground. Looking back, I could see the tall birch trees we'd just walked through. On the right, the beach continued for another couple of yards before morphing into a collection of rocks and boulders. Further ahead, those rocks and boulders gave way to what looked like the start of a mountain. The rocks at the base of it were jagged and wicked looking...almost sinister, I'd say.

It was a tall, imposing monolith, one that we'd never be able to climb over—a total dead-end for us. "A big fuckin' triangle," I muttered, as understanding settled in. I mused that if she'd angled it a bit more, I might have taken her meaning.

That only left one direction to explore. I turned to the left, facing the beach that curved inward and whatever secrets it might have held. I waved my hand in that direction. "I guess we've got to go that way."

Turning back, I saw that my companion had sat down at the edge of the forest. Both of her hands were wrapped around her injured thigh, massaging the sore limb. Treated or not, it still had to hurt. Remembering the blood from earlier, I realised it was a minor miracle she had got this far.

I let my hand fall. "Fine, you can stay here. I'll go."

Turning my back to her, I chose a path to walk the length of the beach, close enough to the surf so that the sand was hard under my shoes while high enough to stay out of the waves' reach. A perfect balance acquired and kept—the mark of a successful enterprise.

There has to be someone, somewhere, I thought, feeling desperation start to set in. *All it would take would be just one helicopter, one aircraft hovering over us. Then we'd be saved. Or a boat. Aye, a boat would do. Don't care if it's a dinghy...* Yet no matter how hard I looked and hoped, the open water at my right stayed as empty as the forest behind the sandy stretch of ground.

A light breeze came in from the sea. It wasn't too cold or too warm. In fact, it felt wonderful after those long weeks of the wet heatwave I'd been forced to endure in Switzerland. Truth be told, most of central Europe had been stuck in that too-warm-for-comfort sweaty cesspool night and day for a month. Anyone who didn't have AC in their homes and offices walked around like sleepwalking comatose patients.

I didn't look back once as I made my way along the shore. I knew the woman would be well out of sight by now, what with the way the beach curved inward. I'd have disappeared on the horizon within minutes. That left me alone and in a quiet place. The corners of my lips curled up at that thought as I came to a halt. *When was the last time such a circumstance had happened to me? Ever? Never...?* The only times I could recall such was when I slept, so it may as well have been never.

I started walking again, noticing how my feet didn't sink in the sand as much as before. The beach was shrinking while the sand felt more and more solid beneath me. Small rocks started darting up through the ground while I kept walking forward. I could see them getting bigger ahead of me, up to the point where a large boulder some five feet high hid the horizon from my sight.

It looked easy enough to climb up close, making me wonder at what lay on the other side and what I'd discover perched on its highest point. Smaller rocks made me some handy footholds up its side and soon enough, I found myself on all fours climbing up the uneven surface.

After several long minutes of trying my best to keep my balance, I reached the top. I turned to face the new expanse of horizon ahead of me. The wind caught in my breath at the sight. For an agonising moment, what I saw kept me from breathing.

There was no beach on this side of the boulder. No sign of civilisation either. Just higher, dark rock formations that inched their way towards the sky until they turned into tall cliffs. The very same cliffs we'd been on earlier. Something settled deep in my guts as a realisation dawned on me. It didn't matter if I kept walking along this shore all day long. I'd never find anything more than what we'd already seen. That's the thing about circles. Sooner or later, you always end back where you started.

I was about to go back down when something caught my eye. Something unnatural and metallic that floated in the water right next to the submerged part of the boulder I was on. Between being half hidden beneath the foaming brine and being ensconced in the rock's dark shadows, I wouldn't have seen it had it been any smaller.

Inching closer so as not to slip and fall, I made out that it was a large length of metal, painted white on one side. Its shape was undefined; its edges ragged. But in my heart, I knew what I was looking at. Another piece of debris from the plane, another vital part that had been torn free from the whole. Another relic left behind that helped explain what had happened to the rest of the aircraft I'd been on. Though I wasn't sure where the front half of the plane was, I knew where it wasn't. It was nowhere near safe ground with us or we'd have found it by now.

This last piece of evidence only served to confirm my gnawing suspicions that there was only one place where the rest of the plane could be: out in the drink below me.

As if to confirm my theory, I turned to my right, my gaze losing itself in the hues of blue before me. There was no white wing rising from the water like a shark's tail. No slew of debris floating in the distance. The flat surface of the sea lay empty and undisturbed as the trees behind me, except for the waves building up near the shore. Either Flight SWA 1528 had crashed further than the eye could see or it had sunken into the depths entirely. There were no other explanations.

My legs gave way beneath me, making me sit on that uneven boulder. Everyone else on that flight was dead. The Captain and first mate. The freckled stewardess who'd brought me my meal. All the passengers I'd stepped in front of in the queue. The ones that were already seated when I got on board. The annoying child that'd been crying the whole flight. The air was sucked out of my lungs at that last thought. It refused to come back.

Pangs of guilt passed through me as I remembered the disdain and smugness in my thoughts. That poor child...he was only doing what all children do on airplanes. He didn't deserve to die for it, not a death as grisly as...

The tears came out in silent streams. Deep inside, I wanted to wail but couldn't find the breath to do it. I'd long been a practical person at heart. I didn't believe in gods or higher purpose or whatever bollocks people use to explain the unexplainable. "No fate but what we make" had always been my motto. But in that moment, fate—and the world it had built—felt far crueller to me than ever.

It was a long time getting back. I kept losing myself in busy thoughts. For all anyone knew, my fellow passenger and I had gone down in the drink with the rest. No help was coming anytime soon. So our next decision would be crucial to our continuing survival. That meant a plan had to be made, organisation put into place, priorities given a hierarchy, tasks scaled proper.

The fear, shame and dread I'd felt earlier had ebbed away while I sank back into a familiar mindset. It was almost a relief, really, the prospect of easing back into a routine of tasks that I was good at.

The curving horizon finally revealed the only other survivor of Flight SWA 1528. She was standing up now, that solid piece of wood in her hand. Since she'd regained her second wind, she was busy doodling something in the sand with the tip of her makeshift cane. As I drew closer, I saw her putting the finishing touch on a very large capital 's' that she'd drawn.

She looked up as she saw me approaching, a tentative smile blooming at the corner of her lips. What was left of my contempt for her vanished. She didn't belong here any more than I did. I was struck again by how young she was. In another life, I could have had a daughter her age.

In my career, I'd been the bearer of bad news more than once. In fact, it'd become something of a speciality of mine. But this time, words failed me. It must have shown on my face, by the way her smile faltered. She took a step closer to try and catch my gaze. After a second, I couldn't meet it, so I looked down.

That made my eyes settle on the thing she'd traced in the sand. In large capital letters was SOS—the universal code for "we're all alone and desperately need some help". *If only she knew how true that was*, I thought ruefully. Then again…given how she'd tried to warn me, maybe she did. And maybe that was why she was writing this in the first place.

I held out a hand toward her staff. Taking it the right way for once, she placed it in my waiting fingers. Next to her final 's', I drew out what I knew in my heart to be true of where we were. A body of land, surrounded by water on all sides.

An island.

9

MORNING SWIM

ANNE-MARIE - 02 AUGUST

An island. Of all the places to be stuck in, it had to be an island. And by the look and feel of things, a deserted one.

This place didn't feel familiar in any sense of the word. It felt isolated and dead, but yet fruitful and part of something greater at the same time. No animal life and sparse vegetation on land. And yet there was an animated sea within easy walking distance of the crash site and wasn't that life all the same? And could that be a chance to survive for us?

This was not how I'd envisioned this trip going. I should have been in Stockholm by now installed in what was going to be my home for the next seven months. I was going to stay with Mr and Mrs Birgerson, to take care of their adorable little three-year-old boy, Noah. I'd always had a great connection with children, especially babies and toddlers. And they seemed to gravitate towards me. So, whenever possible, I did my best to leave them happier than I'd found them.

The Birgersons' file at the *Au pair* agency had said that they owned a little house on Djurgården, one of Stockholm's many islands. When I looked it up on the internet, I discovered there was a theme park not that far away, and a zoo. For months, as I worked the vineyards back home, I daydreamed of taking Noah there. Oh, we would have had so much fun! I'd put him in his little stroller, wrap him up in warm clothes, add a little blanket if there was a need for one. Then we'd stroll down along the shore, mingle with the tourists visiting the capital who were putting on their best faces to make him laugh, smile, and beam. *That's where I should be right now*, I thought with an ache in my heart.

Instead, I was looking around at the empty pebble beach, sparse trees and the blue waters that seemed to stretch out far beyond the horizon. Not the kind of island I'd been dreaming of at all.

As I looked down at my SOS, my throat tightened. I'd made it almost as a joke; that's the acronym they always scratch out somewhere in the movies. Now I realised getting one of those seen may be our only hope of ever getting off this island. Yet when I glanced up at the ever-empty skies, I had to accept there was no one to see it.

Now that the morning had passed, most of the clouds were gone. Aside from the odd light grey patch here and there, the sky was stretching out bright and blue. It was the kind of blue that seemed to electrify the whole sky. An ironic contradiction… a sky vibrant with life, hovering over lonely barren ground. And there wasn't the faintest trace of human disturbance in all that blue, not a vapor trail left by a faraway plane, nothing.

I glanced back down at my lousy SOS. We could set this bloody island on fire and it wouldn't do us any good if there was nobody to see it. I wondered if maybe I should have used sticks and stones to create my SOS. That's also something they did in the movies, probably because it was more visible for the camera. It likely would have been for any passing aircraft. I was getting up to go into the forest and grab various branches when something caught my eye in the water...a glint. I looked up at the waves, trying to narrow my gaze to make out its source. Try though I did, I couldn't find it again.

I moved closer to the surf, bringing a hand up to shield my eyes from the sun as I narrowed them. I was sure there was something there. I couldn't have been seeing things... could I? How long did concussions last? My attitude must have surprised my fellow passenger, given how he mumbled something that sounded like a question.

"I saw something," I said, forgetting for a second how my words would be lost on him. While he didn't understand me, he did mirror my behaviour by following my line of sight with his own eyes. Progress made, I suppose. Due to our language barrier, we were going to have to learn to communicate more with our bodies. *May as well start now*, I thought.

I went back to looking for the object but couldn't find it. Had it been nothing more than a ray of sunlight reflecting off the waves? Then I saw it again, not that far from us. "There!" I said, pointing at it. "Something metallic, reflective."

Leaving my makeshift cane on the sand, I took a step forward, then another. The water was cold on my legs but this was too important. It might have been something from the plane, something that could help us.

As I waded farther in, the incline steepened. A few steps later, I had water up to my hips. Despite the cold, my limbs welcomed the chance to exercise once I started swimming. I discovered a strong current trying to push me to the left, making me correct my course accordingly.

That's when I also realised that this sea or ocean wasn't as calm as I'd thought. The further away I got from shore, the stronger the waves grew. Strong, big and relentless, they tried to swallow me whole, seemingly determined to push me back from whence I'd come. I could feel my limbs burning under the strain. And it was getting harder and harder to keep my head above water while pushing through this undulating barrier. Oh well, at least I wasn't cold anymore.

I wasn't far from my destination when a U-shaped piece of metal with a black plastic grip on top made itself known. That shape could only have been a luggage handle. It was so submerged that I would have missed it if not for it bobbing in and out of the surf at irregular intervals. A couple of strokes later, my fingers wrapped around the plastic.

To my relief, I found out that there was a whole suitcase attached to it, a large, heavy one that was either dark blue or black. I knew I'd have a hard time towing it back to shore, but I had to try. Whatever was inside could be useful to us. Who knew where the current would take it if I left it in the water? *Likely the abyss, never to be seen again*, I thought, clinging hard onto the handle.

I turned and began the long swim back to the shore. While it helped a little to have the waves at my back, I kept having to correct my aim while fighting the current. I had to learn to use the momentum of the waves to push me ahead, an exercise in acceptance and surrender more than anything else.

With my increased distance, I could see the whole of the island. I could see the entire length of the beach, see where it morphed into the roots of the mountain I'd woken up next to, see how it curved into firmer ground on the right. Dark grey boulders and moss-covered earth grew steeper and higher, forming the beginning of the cliffs we'd seen earlier that morning. Then the trees sort of morphed into the mountain, as if they were one giant organism rather than two separate entities. Though the trees covered up the crash site, it wasn't hard to pinpoint where it was. Not quite in the middle of the island, no. More like a little closer to the mountain than the cliffs. That there wasn't anything else in sight but untouched, forgotten nature made it easy to find.

When I got to the point where I had my footing back, I half swam, half walked my way out of the sea, dragging the case behind me while using its natural buoyancy to the best of my advantage.

My fellow passenger hadn't moved, just stayed at the water's edge with his gaze locked on me while I shivered my way out of the salted waters and dragged the water-logged luggage onto the beach. The expression on his face was impossible for me to read. His thick eyebrows had drawn closer together, but I couldn't tell if that meant he was worried or angry. Since he didn't seem like the kind of person who spends much time worrying about others, I decided it had to be the latter.

I knew it'd take me a long time to stop shivering, longer still to dry. I just hoped my morning swim had been worth it. Oh, how I longed to go back to the tail and cocoon myself in the blankets we'd left there. But curiosity got the better of me.

Sitting the case down on the sand, I started looking for the suitcase's zippers...only to discover that it was locked. *"Bôrtâ tzouze,"* I muttered as if the old tongue of my region would get it to open. But under the circumstances, a sealed case was indeed a 'nasty thing'.

Back at the crash site, we shared leftovers from yesterday's dinner in silence. I'd brought the suitcase with me. After all that effort, I was determined to get at its contents. While I sipped some water to finish my meal, I looked around for a rock jagged enough to break the lock.

A gruff voice broke the silence, making me look up to see the man standing up. He was looking away from me, towards the fourth direction that we had yet to try. It wasn't hard to guess his intentions. He wanted to go and explore, see what he could find.

The morning swim hadn't done my leg any favours. Besides, I was too tired to move that far. Despite the two blankets I had wrapped around myself, I was still wet and shivering.

"Don't worry," I said, my fingers narrowing on a suitable rock. "I'll be here when you come back." As usual, the comment was lost on him as he got going without so much as a glance back. I watched him until his thin, lean frame disappeared into the trees.

Returning to the task at hand, I started banging my rock into the small metallic lock. It took me twenty tries to admit that it was a lost cause. The lock was too well-made to break open.

Time for Plan B, I thought, refocusing my attention on the zipper instead. As many an outfit I'd worn could attest, they were far more vulnerable to being torn apart. This time, it only took a couple of hammer blows to the plastic teeth for it to come loose. Feeling the same tingle of excitement I did when opening birthday or Christmas presents, I finally pried the suitcase open.

It contained an assortment of men's shirts and trousers— thick, warm ones, thankfully—along with several pairs of underwear and socks. Since all of it was drenched, I laid them out to dry. Maybe some of it would be of use to my fellow passenger. I wasn't so sure the trousers would fit, since he was rather tall and these a bit too short. But I was certain he could get some use out of the shirts and sweaters.

And if he couldn't, I sure could. Wearing anything warm at all would be a blessing for me. Although the wind was refreshing at times, it got cold during what passed for night time here, with that damn dampness being a constant. We both needed as much insulation as we could scrounge.

There wasn't much else left in the luggage: basic toiletries, a couple of paperbacks that had to be in Swedish, a water-logged laptop that no amount of rice could save.

I was flipping through the wet pages of Johan Theorin's *Skumtimmen* at random when my fellow passenger came back. He sat down, allowing his skeleton-like frame to melt onto the grass. His panting slowed as he allowed himself to rest. Though he said nothing, I knew what he'd found. His trip had led him to another dead-end of water and nothing-ness. Since his tired face and stooped shoulders spoke volumes, what need was there for words?

Our carvings in the sand had been truer than we'd intended them to be. We were stuck on an island, surrounded by uncharted waters, etched next to a desperate cry for help that no one was going to see. Though this stranger whose name I didn't even know sat down inches away from me, I'd never felt more alone in this world. Then I realized that maybe I could change one of those things.

"My name's Anne-Marie," I said, pointing at myself and enunciating clearly. "Anne-Marie."

He didn't understand me at all, his eyes flashing in something that looked like anger.

I surmised that it must have been the accent. *Might writing it down help?* I wondered. Finding a stick on the ground next to me, I wrote out 'Anne-Marie' in a patch of dirt torn up from the crash. Then I pointed at myself and handed him the stick. Begrudgingly, he wrote out 'Killian' just under my name.

I tried his name out loud, making him despair at my poor pronunciation. He had to say it out loud, repeating himself several times before I got it right, whereas I didn't mind that the way he kept saying my name sounded exotic to my ears.

Regardless, it was a step in the right direction. Some kind of connection, at least.

A LITTLE WALK

ANNE-MARIE - 03 AUGUST

Waking up after what had to be my first proper night of sleep since the crash felt weird. At first, being caught up in that hazy not-asleep-yet-not-quite-awake state made me forget what was wrong. All felt right and cottony, even as a disturbing feeling at the back of my spine nagged at me, telling me something was off. As I became more and more awake, the pieces of the puzzle started to come together. For one, the mattress was way too hard. For another, the light streaming in through the drapes was far too bright for this hour. And the final piece of evidence: someone—a man, I believed—was snoring heavily not too far from me.

The memories finally coalesced into something tangible as I sat up. I didn't need to run my fingers over the synthetic fabric under me to know it was the cabin's carpeted floor. Nor did I need to open my eyes completely to see the light seeping in through the jagged opening of the plane. As much as I wanted to forget about this situation, I couldn't. Reality jabbed me without pity, mercy or remorse.

"Good morning, Killian," I mumbled to the sleeping man

up in the galley. The only reply that came from the back of the tail was more snoring.

I rolled my sore shoulders a couple of times before getting up. When I tried to apply some pressure on my bad leg, it felt like it was handling the strain better. The medicine from the first-aid kit had certainly done its job in kick-starting the healing process. Now I just had to wait for it to close up. Maybe I could go by the beach later and dip it into the ocean. I seemed to remember that saltwater healed wounds. Or was that sugar? I wasn't sure either way, but thought it wouldn't hurt to try.

Ambling out of the plane's decapitated corpse, I took a look at the sun-bathed forest around us. It was every bit as quiet as it had been the day before. If help was coming, it was still a long way away. *Looks like patience is one thing we're both going to have to keep*, I thought. I tried not to think about how many days and nights out here that meant.

After a frugal breakfast consisting of yet another KitKat taken from our dwindling supplies, we moved to the beach. There was no need for one of our peculiar discussions to agree on a destination. I couldn't think of a better place to stay for the day and I was betting Killian couldn't either.

After all, we'd be exposed there. Any ship passing by the island would have a chance to see us. Ditto any small plane or helicopter flying overhead. Besides, being near a natural water source like this just appealed to me. It felt so cleansing and restorative, much like the walks I often took by the mountain rivers back home.

After silently following the trail of yesterday's footsteps

through the trees, we came upon the pebble shore and its flat sea of blue and grey. Though it was seven in the morning, the sun was higher in the sky than I expected. Last night, I'd waited for the longest time to see the sunset before going to bed. I gave up at midnight.

It seemed like the sun never wanted to set in this place. It bathed the world in gentle morning light, on through what should be the darkest hours of the evening. There was something rather beautiful about that, like God or Mother Nature reminding us that we must never lose our hope.

Now shining brighter than ever, the sun revealed a receding tide lapping at the feet of a creamy white beach. The frothy waves had swallowed my SOS whole during the night. Guess I was right about using tree branches and rocks instead.

Killian moved to the breaking waves, crouching down to pour water in his cupped hands before splashing his face with it. I left him to his morning ablution so I could search for broken branches and build another call for help, higher up on the beach that was out of reach of the waves.

When I came back out of the forest with an armload of sticks and branches, my fellow passenger seemed busy cataloguing the contents of our provisions bag, which he'd taken with him. Somewhere, he'd found a fountain pen and he was using it to take notes on a white napkin.

Had it been someone else, I'd have used that pen to scrawl my phone number on it like it was a chance encounter in a bar. But since Killian seemed to have the sense of humour of a log, I thought better of it.

Going by how he sat with his back to the ocean, he didn't seem to be one to appreciate the view either. As I got closer, I realised he wasn't even sitting directly on the sand, but rather on an empty bag that he'd folded in quarters. I smiled at the futile gesture; it wasn't like his pricey trousers weren't ruined already. After spending a night laying down on the mud, no amount of cleaning product would get rid of those stains. Not that there was any cleaning product in sight, but still...

While I dropped my bundle of sticks at my feet, I glanced down at my own attire. I wasn't faring much better than my fellow passenger in that department. My once-blue jeans had seen better days and I didn't mean because of the torn-up leg. It was caked with the mud, the leaves, the branches and whatever else had managed to stick to them. I was amazed that my t-shirt only had a few tears around the midriff. My nose wrinkled as the odour from my body hit my nostrils. Our clothes weren't the only thing that needed a wash. We did too.

Sitting on a rock at the edge of the waves, I began to clean myself by digging at the dirt under my nails and then rubbing my ocean-wet palms on my face. My hair was a mess and I knew that nothing short of a good wash could ever untangle the growing bird's nest of curls, dirt and dead leaves that was forming atop my head.

Behind me, Killian continued with his ration list.

While I was busy dabbing my wound with saltwater while trying not to wince, he came up to me with the napkin in his hand. He pushed the diagram he had drawn in front of my face, which I tried making sense of. Not speaking the language certainly didn't help here.

The easiest part to understand was the numbers, all of

them in single digits. I knew we didn't have much. But if I read these numbers right, we didn't have enough to get us through next week. Somehow, we'd have to learn to hunt and gather materials, to harvest what we needed from nature herself.

I knew some individuals were predisposed to survive and thriving in the wild. But that wasn't us, was it? Since Killian looked like a businessman, I'd say being stranded on a deserted island did nothing to play to his strong suits. And while I spent quite a lot of time outside growing up and knew everything about caring for a vineyard, I was in uncharted territory here myself.

After absorbing the diagram, I nodded at him before acting out the fact that I needed to go get dry clothes, wash and rinse anew. He seemed to understand, shrugging me off with surprisingly less annoyance as he retrieved his list. With our silent discussion over, I took up the walking stick and went off.

There was a slight breeze in the air, refreshing, welcome even. Though I didn't have a thermometer with me, I guessed it must have been close to 25°C today. Or at least it would have been without the wind.

While this day was summer at its best, something told me it wouldn't last. Not this far up North. My thoughts darkened as I felt a countdown start ticking away in the background. My imaginary clock was counting back the days until harsher weather returned to these shores. The problem was, I had no idea what the numbers were, so I wasn't sure how long we really had.

On my way back to the beach, fresh clothes from the salvaged suitcase under my arm, I caught sight of a patch of berry bushes. As I moved closer to inspect them, I realised how I had no way of knowing whether these were poisonous or not. To me, they looked like big, juicy blueberries. I salivated at the sight. Had they been red, I would have absconded. But I couldn't, for the life of me, remember ever hearing about purple ones that were toxic. *But maybe I was wrong about that*, I thought. *Besides, how many berries does it take to kill an adult? One, a dozen, twenty?*

My stomach, obviously sick of Kitkats, rumbled, goading me into trying them. I grabbed three and wolfed them down. *Guess we'll know how good they were in a couple of hours*, I thought, wondering if I'd made a mistake.

Committing the bush's location to memory, I continued on towards the beach. When I got there, I found Killian nodding off, his back leaning against a tree trunk. If the marked-up napkin covering his eyes was any indication, he was done doing the maths on our survival.

Moving closer to the waves, I took off my sneakers before adding my pants and shirt. I kept my underwear on—for my benefit or Killian's, I didn't know—and jogged into the foamy sea.

The sunlight reflected off the waters in a beautiful way, showing off a prismatic white light which, in turn, showered upon me. Although quite freezing, these waters got the job done in terms of washing off the encrusted dirt from my body. It didn't take long for me to feel clean again. When I was done, I walked out of the surf and found the dry clothes I'd left on the beach.

My one regret was how there was no way for me to wash off the salt. A fine saltine sheet lingered on my skin as I shrugged on a stranger's cargo pants and T-shirt. The khaki pants were a little wide around the hips, so I tucked the bottom of the beige shirt inside it.

A glance up towards the forest showed me that Killian hadn't moved a muscle. Aside from the cold, I felt fine. No dizziness, no stomach ache; it looked like the berries were agreeing with me so far.

To test the state of my health further, I decided to stretch my legs a little and get my blood pumping. With sneakers back on my feet, I walked the shoreline, the mountain at my back. Beneath my tread, the sand soon became pebbles, and then those pebbles became rocks. When the rocks grew into boulders, I climbed up them. While the hike was hard on my injured leg, it felt invigorating. Frankly, it felt good to be doing something aside from sitting around.

Around a particularly large boulder, I found a small tide pool. Oval in shape, it had to be about three metres wide and six, maybe seven metres long, with a depth of nearly sixty centimetres. All in all, it was nothing exceptional...if you ignored the three fish happily swimming about in it.

"Well, hello, you guys," I said, bending down to look at them with a critical eye. "I baptise thee Breakfast, Lunch, and Dinner." They certainly looked tastier than that dried up salmon Swedish Airline insisted on serving us mid-flight.

Still, I wondered at how I was going to catch them. Since there was no shop selling fishing gear close by, I'd have to make my own. Thankfully, in such a small tide pool, a good spear looked like it would do the job.

I looked about me but found nothing to make one. While there were rocks everywhere, there was no wood to be seen. Having no idea when the high-tide was due, I couldn't chance going back to the crash site for more supplies.

Looking at the walking stick I held in my hand, I weighed my available options. Ease of walking versus a good dinner... yeah, it was no choice at all.

Sharpening the bottom of the stick on a jagged rock was the easy part. Spearing the fish with it, not so much.

"Slippery buggers," I muttered when I missed for the third time.

Breakfast, Lunch and Dinner had become frantic in the small pool. Feeling their impending doom, they zipped left and right at random, each going in a different direction to add to the confusion. In this low depth, their tails stirred up the silt, making the water murky. By attempt number ten, I had all but lost track of Breakfast and Dinner.

Turning all my attention on Lunch, I took a deep breath, narrowed my eyes on the little devil, relaxed my fingers, and —jabbed!

And missed...again. The black shadow had dodged my weapon at the last second.

"*Âlâ piè!*" I had thought this would be easy, but this was turning into a test of my patience and nerves. For some reason, the old tongue spoken by my grandmother and some village elders resurfaced. There weren't many people left who spoke the *Patois Valaisan* anymore. I supposed in a generation or two, it would be all but forgotten. But at that moment, as I fought the wilderness one-on-one, it felt like a fitting language to use.

"*L'ê môrô,*" I tried cajoling him in the old tongue, as I readied my spear for another jab. "*Vin avoui mè...fira onna promenâde,*" I sing-songed. *Come with me for a little walk.* To my absolute lack of surprise, Lunch remained unimpressed with my sweet lies.

The sky had grown darker—though not quite night—when I finally returned to the beach. Killian was nowhere to be seen. I didn't walk back to the camp alone: Breakfast, Lunch and Dinner came along, impaled on the tip of my makeshift spear.

And the good news didn't end there. I felt fine. In fact, more than fine, if positively famished. I took that to mean that the berries weren't poisonous, so I stopped by the bush on the way back to eat a couple more. After pushing some berries into my cargo pants pockets, I followed the footpath back to the broken tail.

I found my fellow passenger seated on a broken trunk, a half-eaten KitKat in his hand. If he'd been worried by my long absence, he didn't let it show. Instead, his attention was focused on my three little friends. For just a moment, I swore he almost smiled.

While I cleaned the fish, he got a fire going. I wasn't sure what these were, but they weren't big. Some kind of mackerel, maybe? I'd done my fair share of trout fishing back home, but when it came to saltwater fish, I was out of my depth, so to speak. Well, fish was fish, and my method of preparing and cooking them seemed to work just as well on them. Once I'd emptied out the innards, I cooked them over the fire with my spear, the skin still on them.

Turns out, Breakfast, Lunch and Dinner were quite tasty. Their flavour was reminiscent of tuna, which worked wonders in terms of gelling with the taste of the blueberries. We'd have to check the pool again tomorrow, maybe look along the coast for other fish-traps if that one was empty.

Who knows? There may also be other berry bushes somewhere else on the island.

The entire time I was eating, I couldn't keep the smile off my face. On second thought, maybe this island wasn't as barren and deserted as I'd first thought. There was life here too, which meant there was hope for us after all. That night, I fell into a deep sleep, filled with dreams of hope and prosperity for our future.

THOUGHTS OF HOME

ANNE-MARIE - 04 AUGUST

The next morning, we awoke to low-hanging clouds and thick humidity in the air. As this wasn't a day for spaghetti tops, I kept my sweatshirt on, even as I caressed the hope that the sun would come out later.

Before we left for the beach, I fashioned two sturdier spears out of thick branches. When I gave one to Killian, I was rewarded with a dubious raise of his bushy eyebrows. Going down to the beach meant walking through the trees and scrubs on what was slowly turning to be a comfortable footpath. We'd been going back and forth so much in the past couple of days that the terrain was beaten and easy to follow. The humidity clung to us as we walked through it, even as the mist remained, clinging to everything below knee-height.

The sound of the waves grew louder as the trees parted. There was no ship in sight on that vast ocean of blue, but at this point, I no longer expected one. Glancing down at my wooden SOS sign, I feared my efforts had been as in vain as the one I'd etched onto the sand.

My gaze returned to the ocean and I lost myself to its vastness and power for a few moments. It was agitated today, pulsing louder than usual as it sent its waves to crash at our feet. As I looked on, something colourful caught my eye. Was it...yes, another suitcase! Not wasting time, I ran to the shore even as I started removing my clothes. We couldn't risk the current sending it away again.

I was in the freezing surf less than a minute later. While the cold had been expected, I was surprised by the strong undercurrents pulling at me as I left the shore. The further out I went, the stronger and more treacherous they grew. It became a struggle just to maintain my course. Still, I was able to force myself to keep my head out of the water so as not to lose sight of the suitcase. Thank God it was bright red with white polka dots. Had it been darker like the first one, I may have lost it in the waves. My arms started to cramp when I reached it, making me glad for the strong waves that carried me and my cargo back to the shore.

The currents kept trying to push me towards the rocks and boulders on the right, but I fought them off while zeroing in on Killian, who was waiting in the sand with spears in hand. He took the suitcase from me when I reached the shore, working to get it open while I hastened to put on warm clothes. Despite my exertions, I felt my teeth rattling hard while my arms shook. Now more than ever, I wished that the prison of clouds would release the sun.

In comparison to the last suitcase, this one opened quite easily. Inside, we found a collection of women's clothes as well as other female essentials. While I would have little use of the frivolous underwear, I knew I could put the assortment of socks, jeans and T-shirts to good use. The week's supply of tampons and pads would also come in handy.

When Killian moved some of the stuff around, my heart clenched at the sight of what was underneath the clothes. Two more T-shirts and another pair of jeans—all of them children's size. Reality caught back up with me at that moment, reminding me once more of all the passengers who hadn't been as lucky as us. I couldn't remember most of them, save for the fellows who'd been sitting closer to me. But I knew there'd been several small children onboard, a wailing baby somewhere near the middle of the plane.

Killian placed the children's clothes back where he'd found them before closing the suitcase completely. A look at his pale face told me that his thoughts had taken a similar path to mine. I inched closer to him. I could have done with a hug right now, but since he didn't seem the hugging type, I forced myself to get a grip.

A cramp ran up and down my bad leg, making me rub it with my hand. With a perturbed look, Killian pointed at the case, then at his chest, then back at the forest. I got the message. He wanted to take the new case back to the crash site. I nodded to let him know that I understood before he turned on his heel and disappeared down the trail. I watched him go, back ramrod straight, white hair standing out in the sea of green. *Such a strange man*, I thought, not for the first time.

After he'd gone, I reflected on how, without some serious effort on both our parts, we wouldn't be able to understand or comprehend one another. That would require ingenuity and patience to get our respective meanings across, something I doubted Killian had much of. I couldn't shake the feeling that my young feminine vigour, coupled with the fact that I was carrying both our weights, threatened his masculine superiority complex. If that was the case, I couldn't have cared less. He was my ally in this battle for survival, so he ought to do his part. There was no other way if we both wanted to live.

Once the cramp was worked out of my leg, I trekked along the shoreline to the pool I found the day before. I prayed the tide would be similar to yesterday's. Spear in hand, I felt like Tarzan hunting Sabor the leopard as I hopped from boulder to boulder. A song in the old tongue drifted through my head as I searched for the tide pool. Along with the song came memories, flowing close as if carried by the waves on my left.

My father's mother used to look after me when I was a kid whenever both my parents were busy in the vineyards. That song was the one she used to sing to lull me to sleep. If I closed my eyes, I could picture her with her knitted purple shawl around her shoulders, her neatly combed grey hair. She had deep lines in her face, drawn more by grief than age. She'd lost her husband in WWII, her youngest daughter to a childhood illness, her eldest daughter to breast cancer at the age of thirty-five. Grandma was the one who'd insisted I learned some local patois, because, as she liked to say, "Some things were not to be forgotten".

Though I hadn't heard the song in years, the words drifted back to me. *Tzantin Tzamozard* was an old ballad about our village's pride: its white wine. While some people may think it a strange topic for a child's lullaby, winemaking ran deep in our community. It was practically etched into our DNA, to the point where many would have said it was Pinot rather than blood that ran through our veins.

In this strange place, lost outside time, it felt good to sing that old song again. If I closed my eyes, I could see the old vineyards on the hills, with their red and yellow grapes soaking in the sun as the green leaves swayed in the wind. I wondered if I'd ever see such things again.

On my way back to the crash site, with a medium-sized cod for a prize, I wondered what Killian had been up to. Hopefully, he'd thought of laying out some new clothes to dry from the polka-dot case. Knowing him, I bet that was the last thing he'd be doing. He was more likely rationing out the berries or building us a sundial to be sure we were always on island time.

That thought led me to wonder where we were exactly. Though we'd been flying over Sweden, this definitely wasn't the mainland. An island somewhere in the ocean north of Scandinavia? But the local temperatures felt way too kind for that. Did the Arctic Circle get this warm in the summer? I knew we weren't as far north as Greenland, but...

That's when I remembered reading how some of Norway's islands were right on the Gulf Stream path. As a result, they enjoyed much warmer weather than was typical for such latitudes. So maybe that was where we were. I would have liked to ask Killian what his thoughts were on that, but it was too difficult a question to mime or draw.

Upon my return to the crash site, I presented the speared fish to Killian. With a smile, I twisted the stick it was on between my hands, like one would before getting a fire set up. In response, he revealed two plastic water bottles with the top cut off. Each of them were filled with an equal amount of berries. While he kept one for himself, he handed me the second. I smiled a little wider. *Even halves*, I thought. *Why am I not surprised?*

After we got a fire going, we cooked and ate in companionable silence. By the time we finished eating, the sky was finally growing dim. And in a place where it never gets dark, it wasn't even in the middle of the night. That was worrisome.

On top of that, the wind picked up, soon followed by the rumble of thunder in the distance. A storm was brewing on the horizon. All the sunny days had lulled me into a false sense of security. I realised now that we weren't equipped to face bad weather. Going by the look on Killian's face as he stood up—a concerned expression stretching his tired, stubble-covered face—he must have been thinking the same thing.

NIGHT STORM

KILLIAN - 04 AUGUST

There was a storm coming. God only knows how long we had until it broke. We'd have to stay the night in the tail, along with everything we'd gathered. I motioned to Anne-Marie to help me grab all our stuff and take it inside. She nodded her understanding and got up without a word.

We hastened to get our bags and belongings as deep into the tail as possible to keep them dry. That meant pushing everything into the back of the galley. We'd worry about making sleeping arrangements later.

On our last supply run into the tail, the first rain droplets hit, thick and heavy. The ground was quick to turn to mud beneath our feet, dousing our fire in seconds. As I hauled myself into what was left of the plane, the wind picked up and pushed the rain inside. That wasn't good. With the way the plane was inclined, along with the gaping mouth of the cabin higher than the back of the tail, water would drop in and pool at the back of the galley. We couldn't risk that happening while we slept. We needed to find a way to stop the water from coming in.

Anne-Marie seemed to have caught on to that too, judging by the pile of blankets she had in her hands. I pointed at the blankets, pointed at the opening and shook my head at her. As heavy as the rain was coming in, they'd be drenched in no time. Anne-Marie's smile told me that she'd thought of that too. After passing me the blankets, she then started to empty the suitcases.

With frantic motions, she pointed to the gaping entrance and the blankets in my hands. I had no idea what she meant. She tried again, a little slower this time, first pointing at the blankets and then at the top of the cabin, near the jagged opening. *Ah, she wants me to fasten the blankets on the juts,* I thought. *Where the bloody hell else could you have hung them out, Killian?*

I did as I was told, placing the pile down by my feet and reaching for one blanket to hold up. The jagged opening was so riddled with pieces of torn metal, it made it easy to prick the thick tissue of the blankets with them. Though the blankets held on, the way the wind was blowing was sure to lift them within the hour. We needed something to hold it in place

I jumped out of the plane and into the slush of dirt and grass. The ground squished and slurped around my shoes as I looked about for small branches. Darkness had all but swallowed up the midnight sun, the woods creaking as the wind roared through them. I stumbled and lost my footing more than once while I ran my fingers through the swaying grass.

The forest looked dangerous and impregnable now, creaking and groaning in the face of the wind storm. When lightning struck, it made the trees seem colossal and grotesque with shadows both thick and primeval. I froze in my steps, unable to tear my eyes away from the sombre sight.

It reminded me of younger days and another forest made of towering giants. Oak, ash, fir and, of course, Scots pine... they roared in the high wind too, extending their long arms over a frightened child. Compared to what I was seeing here, that felt like a lullaby now.

Lightning struck again, the echoing rumble tearing me out of my stupor. "Get a grip, old man," I muttered to myself. Now was not the time to revisit that particular haunt of bad memories. I couldn't bring myself to admit that the time would never come for that.

When I returned to the tail, I was drenched and shivering. Anne-Marie, who'd been busy fastening the suitcases against the bottom of the entrance, scarcely looked better. Her curly mop of hair was matted to the sides of her face, cold droplets dripping out of the long, brown strands. After installing one suitcase in the proper spot, she helped me inside through the gap that remained. I motioned to the branches in my hand, trying to explain what I intended to do with them. It took me three tries for her to get the message. But once she did, she got up to help me.

Soon, the same protruding metallic shards that held the blankets in place were buttressed by an assortment of branches and bits of bark. It was crude work, certainly didn't look like much. But the blankets held on, which was all that mattered. Once that was done, Anne-Marie closed the last gap at our feet with the second suitcase. I gave it a critical eye. As barriers went, it was far from perfect and had holes here and there. But it'd keep most of the water outside.

When I turned to face Anne-Marie—or rather, the place where I thought she was—I noticed how it also kept what was left of the sunlight outside too. The interior of the tail had gone pitch-black. And I couldn't remember what we'd done with that lighter we found in the first suitcase.

"Anne-Marie?" I asked out loud, hoping an answer from her would help me pinpoint her location.

The answering 'hmm, hmm,' came from further inside. It sounded like she was in the galley. Moving forward at a slow, cautious pace, I bumped into her past the *cludgie*. Drawing nearer, I stepped onto something that may very well have been her foot while she elbowed me in the ribs.

"Sorry," I muttered, covering the sound of her apology.

I was about to say more when a flash of lightening burst in through the gaps in the blankets. It was soon followed by the crack of thunder exploding in the distance and the sound of tree limbs crashing to the ground.

Blood turned to ice in my veins. All that took me back to the last time I'd heard thunder exploding in the sky. I could feel myself back on board, tossed left and right as the Captain continued to navigate the treacherous and unfriendly skies. Was lightning going to hit us again? Could we get hurt if it did? I had no idea and that scared me even more.

Anne-Marie must have been thinking along the same lines, as she hadn't moved away from me. Close as we were, I could hear her laboured breathing in the dark.

"It's going to be ok," I said, though I felt more than uncertain. I wasn't sure who I was lying for: my unfortunate companion or myself.

It seemed to do the trick, though. One of her hands found my shoulder and she patted her way down my arm. Grabbing my wrist, she tugged until we both reached the back of the galley. She left me in one corner and I heard her move to the other side before sitting down.

I imitated her, patting my way around the various clothes and supplies until I found a space large enough to sit upon. Then I moved things out of the way, using what I was fairly sure was a sweater as my pillow.

Between the sounds of the storm raging outside and the cold, wet wind that seeped through the wall of blankets and suitcases, finding sleep was a lost cause. Had I been a religious man, I may have even been tempted to utter a prayer or two. But I wasn't, so I settled for staying awake and monitoring the situation, laying in the dark in the hopes of making it to the morning.

13

A PLACE TO CALL HOME

ANNE-MARIE - 05 AUGUST

Though the rain had stopped sometime before we woke up, clouds hung low in the sky. They were charged and dark, seemingly ready to open the floodgates on us again.

Jumping out of the cabin's jagged mouth, I landed in rain-soaked earth and groaned as my trainers sunk in the mud. A second later, a large smile bloomed on my face. Yesterday, I'd been concerned that our water bottles were running low. Now, I realised we'd found our much-needed fresh water source. It was all around us; on every tree leaf, in every muddy pool. What originally had been a major problem would become a life-saving solution in no time.

With two empty water bottles, Killian and I went from leaf to leaf to collect the droplets that had gathered upon them. It was slow-going but felt a little like morning meditation in a weird poetic way. Once our bottles were full, we gulped them down heartily, before repeating the process. We did this about four times.

Compared to what had happened both yesterday and last night, the entire process was a delightful way to start our morning. Killian seemed to be enjoying the peace. Or at least accepting it. Well, maybe *tolerating* it, for lack of a better term. Regardless, he seemed to be going with the flow. Our movements became like a dance through the forest. We waltzed from tree to tree, mindful of where the other was, united in a common goal. And, like the water we harvested, we flowed from leaf to leaf.

As we carried on, a thought occurred to me that we needed to set up receptacles to collect some more of this water the next time it rained. As help clearly wasn't coming, we couldn't afford to waste more potential resources. Optimistic though I could be, even *I* didn't see us fishing out a third suitcase any time soon.

As we sat down on the beach for a Kitkat breakfast, a steady wind kept blowing at us, coming from the waterfront. There was little doubt that the warm temperatures wouldn't hold for long. No matter where exactly we were, it was farther north than I'd ever been. I bet that autumns and winters here could give Switzerland's capricious weather a run for its money. Seeing as we were in the Arctic Circle, we had to be ready for when winter came. That meant our best chance at surviving it would be to keep warm and sustain ourselves through it.

That also meant we couldn't keep sleeping outside or cramped up in the tail. No, if we wanted to survive more dire weather, what we needed was a proper shelter. And no-one but us was around to build it. Other than the very fundamental basics—roof, floor, four walls—I knew absolutely nothing about architecture. While I had my doubts that Killian knew more than I did, it didn't hurt to hope...or ask.

After breakfast, I motioned for Killian to follow me to the wet sand. Once there, I drew my best approximation of a rudimentary shack. He was quick to take the branch from me and to sketch his version of a proper cabin. So he *had* been thinking about it too. Granted, his was much more... exquisite. But it didn't look very doable with what resources —or lack thereof—we'd accumulated.

What we needed out of any shelter was simple functionality. We didn't need it to be luxurious, just safe, dry and warm. I hoped Killian would understand and respect that, rather than let his raging emotions be offended in any way by it.

But before we went into architect mode, we had to find a place to build it on. I drew what we'd come to know as the pictogram for "island" in the sand—an undefined oval-ish shape surrounded by horizontal wavy lines—before placing a question mark in the middle. It had seemed simple and direct enough to convey the question.

Seeming to get my message, Killian stood up and started looking around. Having given some thought to this myself, I decided that had to be dictated by the terrain. No matter what kind of lodging we were going to build, we'd have to dig and plant some support beams if we wanted it to last. The softer the ground, the easier that task was going to be. Then again, the softer the ground, the flimsier those beams would be. Balance was essential. Getting that notion through to my partner wasn't something I could draw with stick figures. So, pantomime it was.

I reached for the hem of his sweater to get his attention. He reacted to this in an extreme way, as always. He acted like he was wondering why I was even touching him, never mind grabbing him so forcefully. But since I'd gotten his attention, I pointed at the ground beneath my feet before miming shovelling. Killian's eyebrows drew closer together as he watched me with an uncomprehending face. How could he not understand what I was doing? What else could he have thought I was...?

I moved to the beginning of the forest, pointed at the ground, and repeated the action. This time I made the shovelling motion seem more difficult and even stopped mid-swing to wipe imaginary sweat from my brow. Damn, but this was starting to feel like a game of charades.

As I jogged back to Killian, I could see him trying to make sense of my actions. His face had this lost-in-thought quality to it, as opposed to his typical irritated expression. But was he trying to understand my message or was he working on the solution already? While I truly hoped for the latter, it could have equally been either or none, knowing him.

He moved back to the spot where I'd made my second mime-session, bending down to inspect the soil. Then he stood up and walked further into the woods. Ten steps into the forest, he did the same thing before going another ten steps further. Then he came back to where I'd been waiting.

He motioned to the ground again, and his gesture had a finite quality to it. "There," it seemed to say as if he'd made up his mind, matter-of-factly.

I gave him my version of a puzzled look. He bent down to grab a reluctant fistful of dirt, bringing it up for me to inspect. On his wrinkled palm, I discovered a mix of dirt and sand that only existed in this very spot, right where the forest ended and the beach started. A surface that was neither too hard to dig into, nor too loose to support the beams...perfect balance.

This length of mixed soil, where green grass grew amidst the golden grains of sand, ran all along the beach, maybe two or three metres wide at best. Nothing big, but wide enough to hold the small shelter that we aspired to create.

There was one glaring drawback to this unprotected location. This far outside the forest, the wind would hit us pretty strongly. *But at least the view here would be nice,* another part of my brain supplied. Keeping with that train of thought, I wondered if we couldn't build it closer to the mountain. Such a tall structure might offer us some shelter from the elements.

I started walking that way and, after an exasperated sigh, I heard Killian follow. It was a short walk to the mountain's base. Come to think of it, everything here was a short walk. But the ground held a mean surprise. Gone was the dark brown dirt; rocks and stones ran sinuously beneath our feet. I grimaced at the sight. It'd be a nightmare to try to dig through here. Besides, the stones were way too big to hold any support beams in place. I sighed with disdain as I slapped the sides of my head.

As I turned my back on the tall mountain, Killian gave me a "What were you expecting?" kind of look, which I chose to ignore. I kept looking at my feet on the way back and stopped walking the moment I was sure the ground was good again. Glancing over my shoulder, I saw that we had to be some five hundred metres from the mountain. It was tall enough to still do the job of blocking or at least tempering any winds coming from that direction. The trees would do the same on the left. We were in a sweet spot of sorts.

Clearing our future sleeping area was easy enough. We removed all the branches and rocks we could find, making sure the surface was as smooth as can be. Then—mostly for fun—I twirled around in circles and broke any little branches that might have been uncomfortable, like a wild dog or cat before they lie down and get some sleep. I smiled at Killian while I did this, which got me a roll of his eyes. He *would* keep to a more serious tone about this.

As we worked, I kept trying to remember everything I knew about building a shelter in the wilderness. There were many ways to go about it. With the right kind of power tools and manpower, I'd happily have fashioned a nice log-cabin with separate rooms, maybe even an upper-floor. But since it was just the two of us with a limited assortment of metallic debris to use as knives, hammer and nails, we'd have to keep it simple but sturdy. That meant four walls and a roof that would have to somehow hold together. Our survival depended on keeping the fundamentals in mind and in heart.

I went camping a lot when I was a child. Our village was perched on the side of a mountain, so it didn't take much of a hike to be in the wilderness. As soon as my parents deemed me old enough, they let me go with my cousins to the *Vérines* —a settlement higher up on the mountain.

With my brother and cousins, we used to follow the foot trails up for a thirty-minute walk, gorging ourselves on some unobstructed views of the entire length of the Rhone Valley —from Sion to Martigny. We'd hike upwards until we'd reach the *Colline aux Oiseaux* campsite—"the birds' hill". It was aptly named too, given its height and the large number of birds we'd see there every time we went. That reminded me of one thing that was sort of strange and eerie about this island: if there were birds, we hadn't seen them yet. At all. Were we that far out from the continent?

It made me shudder to think that, so I got back to thinking of the *Colline* and its quaint little restaurant where the owners liked to play the accordion in the afternoon. At an altitude of over 800 metres, the camping and its restaurant sat next to an artificial circular basin, where the trout roaming the water were easy to catch. In the summer, that basin became the delight of many a tourist with zero fishing skills. For a small fee, they could even borrow the needed fishing equipment on site.

My cousins and I had a habit of camping in the forest between the village and the campsite, in a small clearing close to the footpath. Though we had tents and camping equipment, we often tried building our own shack. While we never really succeeded, it passed the time and fit in our narrative of kids facing the wilderness.

As I looked at the spot Killian and I had cleared, I wished we had some tarp and rope. It would be easy to make a shelter with those. But like so much else, we had none of that. The two things we had in spades were time and despair.

14

ARCHITECTURE 101

ANNE-MARIE - 05-08 AUGUST

The best way to build something is from the ground up. That was a basic tenet of carpentry...wasn't that what it was called? Regardless, we needed some kind of framework for our shelter. While wood was certainly something we had in abundance, we were a little short on chainsaws and axes. So we'd need to make our own cutting implements.

I remembered how the tail-end of the plane damaged some of the surrounding trees when it crashed. With gestures, I got through to Killian that we could try to gather some of those broken branches. Really, though, any sturdy stick we could find might prove useful.

As we left the mountain and beach behind us, heading back to the tail, I found myself feeling for the Earth. It was quite tragic, the way this artificial metal bird had scraped her flank and left a large tear in her belly. Not that it had stopped her natural glory but I'm sure she'd felt the wound. Too many people think of the Earth as an inanimate object. But she feels everything...every scar, every rupture, every release.

Maybe it was a blessing to her that we were the first two humans to ever set foot on this spot.

Back at the crash site, we began sorting through the disembodied branches of two of the broken trees by size. The largest went into the left pile, mediums in the middle, with the smallest being stacked on the right. Well, I say that "we" had begun the sorting when it was actually just me. I found it a bit funny how little old me was the one doing all the heavy lifting while Killian busied himself with drawing up design plans. Come to think of it, I'd wager I was stronger than him, pound for pound. With that skinny frame and clumsy energy, he wouldn't have managed more than a few minutes of this work. Not an insult to him, but it was likely true.

Besides, his self-appointed job suited him rather nicely. He scribbled away on his napkins with a passion, pausing at times to consider his next move before diving back in again. It looked as though we had both discovered our niches. I was the muscle, he was the brains. With a smile, I kept sorting out the mess our plane had made of the local forest.

Some of the branches I found were quite dead, not suitable at all for being part of a foundation of any kind. At best, they'd simply break under the pressure of a roof. At worst, they'd break as soon as we attempted to put them into the earth, so I stuck to others that were much sturdier and full of fresh sap.

I sorted them out until all that was left were the two bare tree trunks and the largest branches. All of them were much too heavy to carry by myself, which didn't stop me from trying numerous times. Yet, even with all my might, I hadn't been able to make those trunks move so much as an inch.

But I had hopes that the branches could be moved, provided I had some help.

Returning to Killian's drawing spot, I stopped to gulp down some water. Before I got his attention, I peeked over his shoulder to see what he was drawing. His architectural concepts sure were beautiful...and completely unfeasible. They included such extravagant bells and whistles like a skylight, which would only let the rain in worse than the hole in the tail had. It was one of many pointless 'extras' that would be more of a problem than a solution to my eyes. Poor Killian...I'm sure he lived in some fancy penthouse in a big city somewhere, but luxuries in the city were liabilities out here. Guess he didn't know what that was like to come from a humbler background—or so his architectural fancies seemed to imply.

Tapping him gently on the shoulder, I motioned for him to give me the pen, which he reluctantly did. Reaching for a blank napkin, I quickly traced the outline of a much more realistic shelter. It used part of one of the large trunks I needed his assistance with as well several pieces of the plane I was fairly certain we could detach.

When he saw my design, I could tell that me correcting him had hurt his pride a little. His lip involuntarily curled downward, a sort of reflex in reaction to feeling the pain of inadequacy, which he bit into to stop. I shrugged my shoulders in a 'sorry, but what else could I have done' gesture. This was about survival, not a submission to *Architecture Weekly*. I returned him my new version of our proposed palace in the woods before motioning towards the branches I needed his help with.

Together, we brought our building materials to our spot on the beach. Hauling them over took all morning and half the afternoon. Once we were done, I was parched and famished, but we'd yet to hunt for our food. I gave Killian the gesture we had agreed upon for berries and then mimed that I was going to try to find us some fish.

The next morning was spent manufacturing the basic tools we'd need to cut and trim the assorted branches. We broke up medium-sized stones on larger boulders. The largest pieces would be used to carve out branches and large chunks of thick bark. The rest could be turned into a sort of pre-hardened concrete, which would help seal the support beams into the ground. I had to admit that this last had been one of Killian's most brilliant ideas to date. That mesh of stone debris would keep the pillars wedged into the earth, able to stay strong through even the fiercest of windstorms.

It took us the entire morning to get four of those stones broken, sharpened and ready for burial. The bad part was that wasn't even half of what we needed. Once again, the remainder of the afternoon was spent doing the rest until it was time to stop and hunt for our supper.

By now, I had a sense of the tides' timetable. Consequently, I knew how long I had until the waves swallowed the tide pools and freed the fish that may otherwise be trapped within.

That night, I returned to the camp with two cod that we roasted over the coals. It tasted a lot like yesterday's meal. And the one before that. But food was food. Much like Killian's proposed skylight, menus were a luxury we currently didn't have.

We selected the thicker and most linear branches we'd found to use as support beams. We readied them by trimming off their bark and removing the biggest knots. The branches were cut to a length of about one metre fifty. With fifty centimetres firmly planted in the ground, that would leave us with one-metre in support beams all around.

Speaking of which, the next step was actually planting them in the ground. I had no idea how deep we needed to dig for the structure to stay solid. Like everything else, we were going to have to wing it.

When Killian tried planting the first branch, it only went in a couple of centimetres. Since that wasn't enough, we took it out and started digging, using some plane debris that were vaguely circular chunks of metal. We wrapped strips of blankets around our palms so that we wouldn't cut ourselves using these crude tools.

We wound up making the hole larger than needed, leaving some room at the sides for the stones to be wedged into it as well. Once we planted the beams, the stones went in next. We used them to stab the sides of the branches—not enough to break them, just enough to keep them steady— before filling what was left of the hole with a mixture of sand, dirt and water. Thankfully, it seemed to hold after we were done.

By mid-afternoon, we had four branches standing proudly at the corners of a well-defined rectangle. The rectangular shape stretched out two metres long on the narrower side and three metres on the longest. At these lengths, we'd both be able to sleep with our entire bodies stretched out comfortably. I doubt Killian wanted a repeat of the cramped conditions of the galley any more than I did.

We planted two more beams in the middle of the longest sides, reserving one to install next to what would be our front door. I knew we had the loo door to use for that, but at this point, I had no idea how to affix that to the structure. *Well, something else we could worry about at a later time,* I thought as I continued to work.

By the end of the second day, my body was on fire. My arms, my legs, my back... So much of me hurt that it was hard to narrow down the exact spots. I had no strength left to go fishing, so that night's *menu de jour* were the last three potatoes we had along with a couple of sachets of that awful dill sauce. And for dessert, of course, half a KitKat.

With dinner over, I started digging out the splinters that built up in my hands over the day's work. Piece after piece, satisfaction seeped its way into me as I removed those wooden parasites from my rough, calloused hands. I breathed heavy sighs of relief while pulling each tiny fragment out of my hands. Killian kept looking at me with a curious, judgemental look, as if it were 'wrong' of me to be enjoying what little pleasure I found in the task. I was too tired to care.

Though he hadn't worked as much as I did, his own hands were no better than mine. If anything, they looked worse. He'd been forced to bandage up the red, abused skin of his palms with more strips of blankets.

After what had seemed like about half an hour of tending to our individual wounds, we made our way back to our tin can shelter for the night.

The next day found me waking up to Killian tearing down and dismantling what was left of the loo door. While the left one was missing, the other had three flimsy hinges barely holding it to the wall. In a rare display of strength and power, Killian ripped it off its hinges. I think the fact that they were torn and mangled beyond repair played a big part in the feat, but I pretended to be impressed just the same. If it put him in a good mood, he could have this little victory. It probably made up for the throbbing I knew was running through his still-bandaged hands.

Getting up, I pondered unhinging all the cabinet doors in the galley, but I didn't see what we could do with those. Maybe there was a way to use them like furniture or storage?

Well, interior decorating was something we could worry about later, I decided. For now, our shack needed the essentials of some walls and a roof. That meant long sheets of flat material. And something to hold it to the support beam we'd planted in the ground. Honestly, I had no idea what we could use as a roof. I hoped Killian had a better one in mind.

As I stood there looking around, my eyes settled on the curved walls themselves. Maybe whatever they were made of could come off? When I moved closer, I discovered junctions between the assembled pieces. Running my fingers along the material, I couldn't figure out what it was made of. While it seemed light and flimsy, it didn't dent when I tried pressing my finger against it.

Yesterday, I'd turned a lengthy piece of debris into something that resembled a chisel, with a piece of cloth tied around the end to serve as a handle. I took it to one of the visible junctions and tried cutting there. The material came away under the blade. To my surprise, it was much thinner than I'd anticipated. Still, it looked sturdy enough, made of some honeycomb material lined with thin protective sheets. All in all, it wasn't much more than a centimetre thick. But no matter how much pressure I put on it, the stuff refused to lose its curved shape at the top. It must have been pressed into shape when it was super-hot. Well, never mind contemporary design—our home's roof could have a rounded look. When in Rome, right?

After some show-and-tell with Killian, we worked at ripping off these panels all along the sides of what remained of the cabin. This time, Killian was the primary physical labourer while I sat down behind him, thinking of some ideas to make them hold together which I jotted down on today's napkin. Personally, I was glad that he gave me this time to rest. After all my efforts in the past couples of days, I needed it—even if I didn't want to admit it to myself.

As I looked at my fellow survivor deftly stripping pieces of lining, I realised Killian was great at tearing things apart. I, on the other hand, was better at putting things back together. I felt like there was a joke in there somewhere. Still, it was interesting to consider.

While Killian ripped up the walls, I finally came up with a couple of ideas. One was that we could try melting them together with however hot a fire we could build. The other was to stab holes in the edges and find some kind of rope to hold them together. Seeing as we were short of rope, while fuel for fire was aplenty, the decision was a no-brainer.

I looked around the walls again as Killian removed the panels, and stopped. There was one solution, at least. The wires dangling from the opening of the plane looked like threads—threads that could be woven into a rope of our choosing, if we wanted to. They were made of many different colours and thicknesses, and—I looked at the space one of the panels used to occupy—they ran the length of the tail, at least as far as I could tell.

I stood up, reaching into the insulation in the wall, and tugged at a wire. It moved, but the ones around it twitched as well—they must be grouped up together further down the line, between this point and the opening. I started exploring with my fingers.

When Killian came back, I showed him the wires, and mimed twisting them together, and then of sewing something. He stared at me for a few seconds, frowning, then nodded. As he worked at the panels, I worked on pulling the wires out of the plane's carcass, searching through the walls for junctions and gatherings that I would need my chisel to cut through.

As I worked, I realised that the wires—blessing that they might be—would not work for the roof – any holes in the moulded plastic stuff would let in the rain, if we didn't crack the stuff trying to drill it with our crude tools. We could save the wires for holding up the walls, and the door, as well as doing something to secure the roof down. No, we would have to melt the roof together, somehow.

I started gathering firewood, small kindling that would be enough to make a torch. Killian soon joined me, his bushy eyebrows drawn up. I'd figured out that it was an unequivocal sign that he didn't know what I was up to now. While I could try to explain, I chose to raise a finger in a 'wait a minute' kind of gesture.

Once the torch was ready, I asked Killian to hold the linings in place. As he stood underneath them, holding two pieces together, I moved by his side with the torch, placing the flames where the slabs met. At first, it did nothing but darken the material with soot. I was all but ready to give up when the edges slowly but surely started to melt.

The technique wound up working like a charm and the time it took to make it fuse was well worth the end result. We would have no problem creating a roof for our new humble abode. I was quite proud of both of us for executing such a unique and brilliant idea, to say the very least.

Once the joined material had cooled off, we carried it to the beach and the skeleton of the house we'd built. Once we'd placed it atop the beams, I was satisfied to see that it was both large and long enough. We still had to figure out a way to make it stay in place, but...one challenge at a time.

Although the shack was far from finished, I felt a swell of pride at what we'd accomplished so far. We had worked together to make this, overcoming and surpassing language barriers—not to mention emotional, mental, and physical barriers—to achieve a common goal. Actually, I was more than proud. I was gratified.

I smiled at Killian as he sat down under our new roof. The way he was panting reminded me that he was much older than me. Maybe I ought not to ask too much out of him. Nevertheless, the smile stayed on my face as I sat next to him and looked up appreciatively. We'd done a good job. The beams protruded from the ground at something close to a ninety-degree angle. Now all we had to do was fasten the damn roof to them.

Looking at it from this angle, I was reminded of what Killian had done during the storm. The shards of metal, the blanket, the pieces of wood to complete the sandwich...could we do something similar here? That's when it hit me.

"We need to drill holes through the roof," I said aloud. "That'll keep the roof in place."

Killian looked at me like I'd sprung another head. *Of course, Anne-Marie,* I thought as I moved to my knees. *Remember that he doesn't speak your language.*

I started drawing on the floor the schematics of what we'd have to do. Making holes through the roof at the exact location where there was a beam, thinning the top of the beams to a length of ten centimetres length, and then *voilà*. So long as we made our holes a diameter larger than the top of the beams yet smaller than the bottom part, the roof would slide into place and stay wedged in. Perfect.

After that, the only thing left to do was to build some walls and a door and we'd be golden. Yep, said like that, it sure as hell sounded easy. My aching body made a point of reminding me that it could be otherwise.

15

ARCHITECTURE 102

ANNE-MARIE - 09-23 AUGUST

Turns out, there was nothing easy about it. Sure, the idea itself was simple enough. Sure, drawing up the schematics and figuring out the right diameters had been a breeze. But taking that idea and turning it into something concrete? Well, that was something else. I was no carpenter and neither was Killian. On top of that, our only working tools were rock-shards and airplane debris.

The only thing we had going for us was that we had time. Plenty of time. Absolute freedom to work from dawn till dusk under an unforgiving sun that never seemed to want to set. Save for the breaks we had to take to collect dew water, spear our dinner from the tide pools and gather berries for dessert, we worked non-stop every day from seven in the morning until seven in the evening per Killian's still-functional wristwatch. We worked in silence, using diagrams to map out our day's work and hand gestures when we needed the other to accomplish a specific task.

Though Killian never said it out loud—not that I could have understood him if he had—strict adherence to a schedule seemed to improve his mood. It was as if he found comfort in the natural routine that established itself after the first couple of days.

But then, my travel companion wasn't the only one who enjoyed having an occupation. Now that we had something to do with ourselves, the days seemed to flow by, as if the world made sense again. Funny how focusing on gruelling manual tasks and working towards a goal grounds you and provides you with a sense of purpose.

It took us three days to get the roofing done, fastening them with stoppers we made out of tight bundles of wires, coiled into rope, to make sure not even the strongest winds could lift it off. Another five days were spent gathering and preparing the materials to make the walls. Four days to affix them to the support beams. One more to install the loo door that'd serve as an entrance to our humble abode.

Day fourteen was spent working on the inside. We gathered leaves to make two mattresses, covering them with blankets until it was as comfortable as any cheap and dingy hotel room's bed. Then came the interminable treks from the crash-site to the shack, bringing along all our stuff. We'd put one mattress against one wall and the other against the opposite one. That left us a little space in the middle to pile up the suitcases that'd washed ashore, along with the rest that we'd salvaged from the tail.

On the fifteenth day, we stayed in bed until mid-morning, planning on not doing anything more than gather up much-needed fresh water and food. I thought it would be the best day of our week, but I should have known better.

Whatever peace of mind Killian had found in our routine was gone by the time he got up. The old man was back to his old grumpy self, all spurts of happiness replaced by displeasure and disdain. When it was apparent that all he was going to do was brood, I decided it would be best for us to split up for the day.

I gave him my spear and motioned a fish swimming in the water with my hands. Though it was my usual job to get the fish and his to pick the berries, he took it without protest. Eyebrows coming together to form a scowl, he stormed out of the shack with grim purpose.

I sighed. *That man*, I thought in despair. It really couldn't be helped though. Nor was it my business or prerogative to. Even so, since we were stuck on a deserted island together, there was nothing else to do but go pick more berries.

I started walking down the path—and off it a little—back to the spot where I had first found the berry bushes. It didn't take long for me to get there. Once I did, I got right to picking.

I couldn't keep my thoughts off from my companion, trying to guess at what was going on through that thick skull of his. Building the shelter together had brought me new perspectives and the realisation that things were easier when we shifted our focus to being constructive rather than destructive.

But I hadn't anticipated that losing the daily schedule we'd gotten used to would affect him so. Must it always be one step forward, two steps backwards with that man?

The morning passed as I bathed and then washed my clothes before hanging them to dry on a branch. When Killian hadn't returned to the shelter three hours later, I started to worry something might have happened to him. Maybe I was being irrational, but I couldn't help it. Half a dozen scenarios worthy of Hollywood Z movies flooded my brain.

What if he had drowned? What if he became stranded on the very same rocks that I had fished at before by a fast tide? Were there sharks this far north? If so, what if one had got to him?

Worrying for the worst was a quality I hated to admit that I had, but had it I did. It was something I'd inherited from my mother. I remember her worrying about my father and me many times as we worked the family business. It's not as if growing grapes was dangerous in itself, but the mountaineering that was involved with some of our higher elevation vineyards was enough to make my mother shudder at the thought of one of us losing our grip.

Deciding to do more than worry, I began walking along the water, feet digging deep into the sand. I should have shied away from the cold feeling of the water, but I'd somehow got used to it. It wasn't that I couldn't feel it anymore, it was just that my mind had found the ability to file away that particular piece of information and discard it as unimportant. Besides, with no bath or shower on this island, daily dips in the waves had become part of our routine to wash away the day's sweat. They also did wonders for numbing the pain caused by a hard day's work, and the occasional bout of rain washed away the remaining salt.

Reaching the boulders, I climbed up them and started jumping from one to the next, helping my body get my blood pumping.

It turned out to be pretty easy to find Killian. I could make out his frustrated shouts at the water and fish themselves from a mile away. That man...

By the time I reached him, he was all but slapping the water with his spear. What he hoped to accomplish by doing that, I had no idea. I giggled to myself as I hopped over to the tide pool. Three hours he'd been at it, with no food to show for it.

All levity aside, this was a problem. We had no over-stuffed larder waiting for us back home, which meant we relied on the daily catch to keep us fed. Killian's attitude was a liability we couldn't afford any more than we could have his architectural fancies. If I let it, his anger would end up being the death of him, me or both. That was something I refuse to let happen.

He looked up at me, his face beet red and bushy eyebrows set low. I held my hand out. He all but slapped the spear into my hand before moving to sit down on a nearby boulder, like a scolded child.

I returned my attention to the water at my feet. Any fish that'd be in the tide pool had been scared away by all the splashing and shouting. It was going to take time to coax them out of their hiding spot. But then, fishing was a game of patience. Spear firmly in hand, I heaved in a deep breath as I centred myself, moving to find a comfortable, balanced position. Focusing on the water below and what was within it, I relaxed as I let go of everything. All my focus was on the glistening pool at my feet, basking in the light of my diligence and dutiful actions through non-action. Sometimes, there wasn't anything more to do but wait.

After about an hour, a couple of medium-sized fish made their way into the tide pool, coming in from a small tributary leading to the sea. Smiling, I tightened my grip on the spear but otherwise remained motionless.

These twin codfish, whom I nicknamed Mine and His, were minding their own business, clueless of the danger looming above them. I breathed in, aimed, locked on, then exhaled and shot the spear downward—a direct hit on Mine.

Predictably, that scarred the bejesus out of His, making him scurry away. Turning on my heel faster than you can say *bouillabaisse*, I readied myself for another shot, eyes locked onto the mouth of the tributary. One breath, two breaths, and His was right in my sights. I threw the spear again and His was reunited with Mine.

When I looked up at Killian with a victory smile on my lips, his face was unreadable. There were so many emotions warring for dominance on his drawn features, it was hard to tell them apart.

On the walk back, his silence and cold shoulder continued while we hopped barefoot across the large boulders. At least he wasn't mumbling any hate spew or letting negativity build up within himself. Surely that counted as a win, didn't it?

When we made it to the sand, Killian had something that he had wanted to show me. He began writing in the sand, a cross-stitch pattern, like the game tic-tac-toe, but with many more rows and columns. Was that…a net?

I smiled at him. That was a great idea. Attracting prey worked much better than chasing them. I'd love for us to work on creating something to catch the fish in, rather than having to go out and hunt them every day.

When we returned to the shelter, Killian took the fish off the spear and insisted that he cook them. I let him. Any way that he wanted to help was fine with me, so long as we survived, thrived, and eventually got to go home.

16

SURF-AND-TURF

KILLIAN - 24 AUGUST

The next day, I awoke to see Anne-Marie tying what looked like some wild fibres together, along with the occasional strand of thin wire we hadn't used on the shelter. Dressed in a beige T-Shirt that proclaimed "Life is better with Choco-late," she had installed herself outside, sitting on a folded blanket against a fallen log.

She seemed to be repeating the same motions over and over again. First making a loop and then entering it with the tip of a second rope from the front. Then she'd wrap that rope around the right outer side of the loop, pull the tip across the front and around the outer edge on the other side before slipping it underneath itself on the back. By the looks of it, she'd used one of the woollen jumpers we'd gotten out the first suitcase as core material, unmaking it and braiding several different fibres and wires together to make them thicker.

As I yawned and looked over at her, the realisation dawned on me that she was making a net. Blood surged in my veins at the sight, blazing through my entire being swift and fierce. I lunged at her. *My idea,* my mind screamed at me; loud and furious. *My. Idea.*

I should have taken a minute to analyse that outburst, sought to understand the insecurities from which it had stemmed. But proud fool that I was, I didn't. I latched onto the anger, feeling comforted by its familiar stupid simplicity.

"What do you think you're doing?" I all but screamed and Anne-Marie flinched at the tone. "That was my idea, *lassie.*"

Turning to face me, the young woman looked gobs-macked as her wild curls bounced back into place. Her round eyes grew larger as she looked up at me, uncomprehending.

Though I knew any shred of understanding between us would be lost in the wind, it was with the same tone and intensity that I added, "Give me that! That's mine! Keep your stupid spear and do what you're good at, ya slag!"

Anne-Marie kept staring at me with that same surprised, hurt expression. There was no understanding on why I'd felt disrespected or belittled. Looking back now, of course she didn't. How could she have? The only thing she ever thought of was what was best for our survival.

And so there I was, fuelled by resentment, unable to see past my own lack of self-confidence and inadequacies, pouring all the coldness I could muster into my stare until she tossed the net my way. Without another word, she got up, grabbed her spear and left.

I didn't watch her go, didn't try to stop her and make amends. I looked down at the beginning of a net that had landed at my feet. After a moment of studying its design, it seemed simple enough to continue. And of course, it was anything but.

Try though I might, I couldn't replicate her resilient

knots. Not even after I'd taken a couple of slow, deep breaths to calm my nerves. Not even after the adrenaline had receded enough that my fingers stopped shaking. I kept getting stuck on the basic crafting. Had it been in and then to the right, or had the yarn tip better come in from the back of the loop before tying it to the left? Because I couldn't remember, I wound up making a mess of what she'd begun. I gave up a couple hours later, tossing the jumbled clutter of wool near the place where Anne-Marie had been sitting.

My fingers ached from all the knot tying I'd been doing— or attempting to do. Even after building our house, my hands still weren't used to manual work. I longed to dip them into something cold and soothing. Standing up, my stiff joints cracking in protest, I started down the forest path, what I'd come to think of as our 'Grand Avenue' to the sea.

On the way to the beach, it struck me how I was alone again. What a strange thought it was too. I couldn't remember the last time I'd felt this alone. Back in my old life, I'd always been conversing with someone or another, striking business deals, arranging staff meetings, making appointments with clients. Now that there was none of that, I felt unsettled...as if I lacked any purpose to remain on this earth.

While I'd never been one to seek company, I was content, between loud open offices and serviced hotel rooms ensconced in bustling cities, with the anonymous companionship that living amongst a human cesspool provided. A life lived at a frantic pace, powered by the constant fear of being left behind. Rushing from one appointment to the next, from cab to subway to plane, the world growing ever smaller, the pace ever faster.

And now, all I had around me was this path of stamped-upon grass, dead leaves crinkling under my feet and a silence that only solitude could provide. My fingers twitched for something to occupy them. I realised how much I longed for my phone, my laptop, to feel a connection to…something, the adrenaline rush that came with taking on a challenge, an impossible deadline that would somehow have to be met. Yet this island had none of those on offer. It was utterly bereft of the one thing humans couldn't live without: purpose.

That thought made me stop dead in my tracks and look around once more. It was a peaceful sight, most would say, lacking anything even remotely manic. It was a world of plain and simple facts, no hidden agenda, no politics, no white lies to get you through the day. Just an endless quiet that should have been a balm to the soul, but that felt like a bushel of thorns in my side.

Had there been times in my life where I wished for some place like this? Sure, too many to count. A little bit of space to breathe, a pause button… A little peace and quiet to take stock. But never had I dreamt of such a hard reset. Was this the universe's way of taunting me, mocking me? By giving me what I had wanted for all these years, not in measured sips but in the most extreme of ways? Was this my own personal hell; tailored to fit me like the business suits I took pride in wearing? If so, maybe there was something to Wilde's thoughts on the gods' punishments coming in the form of answered prayers.

I got walking again, thoughts swirling around like a maddening dance in my head. Then I realised that I'd strayed from the path and done the second fool thing of the day: gotten lost.

"*An donas dubh!*" I cursed out loud.

That old Gaelic outburst flowed from the tip of my tongue without me wanting it to, leaving behind a soothing aftertaste that felt reminiscent of younger years and strong scotch. Even to my ears, the vowels had sounded thick, reminding me how my Scottish accent had grown more pronounced ever since we'd crash-landed on this island.

The footpath that we'd been tramping all over back and forth was nowhere to be seen now. No matter how I searched for it on the left or right, it remained hidden from my eyes. I tried retracing my steps to no avail.

"Now you've fuckin' done it, haven't you, old son?" I said, my worrying increasing with each step. As I kept searching for the path, I found something I hadn't been expecting…a patch of mushrooms! There they were, nestled under a shrub at the foot of a tree. After weeks of fish and berries, they looked delicious.

Kneeling, I picked two dozen of them, using my shirt to carry them. It brought a smile to my face to think that I would be the one adding to our pantry for once. Thanks to me, surf-and-turf would be on the menu tonight. It pleased me to be able to show Anne-Marie that I could be just as useful as she was. It was time she saw that I had something of value to offer to our team.

Careful not to drop them, I tried making my way back to the crash site, whichever way that was…I had no more idea on that than I did the path I was walking. But I wandered on joyfully just the same. Casually, I ate one of the mushrooms. It tasted bitter and dirty, of course, but it still went down with no hesitation. I was sure it would taste delicious once it'd been cooked. After a while, I ate another one while I kept looking for the way back.

Time dragged on and the skies darkened. I wondered if it was because our midnight sun season was coming to a close that today's afternoon looked darker than it had the night before. I kept trying to head in the direction of the waves I could hear in the distance. But the trees began to look more and more sinister. They undulated in the wind as if they had a will of their own. Their warped leaves loomed above me, whispering haunting words over the breeze.

Hurrying up the pace, I felt my breath quicken as I looked for the familiar vision of a white tail peeking through green foliage. It was nowhere in sight, making worry and despair creep up in my guts.

A tree root rose out of the ground, catching one of my feet in its grasp. I stumbled and lost my footing. Falling in heap on the forest floor, amidst a sea of discarded mushrooms, I felt branches and roots digging in my sides. It was as if they were trying to trap me, pulling me under to try and bury me in an earthly grave. Pushing up on my knees and elbows, I tried fending them off.

Before I knew what hit me, Anne-Marie grabbed my arm out of nowhere and pulled me to my feet. The change in stance was jarring. It took me some time to be able to focus on her face. I noticed that she looked worried. She was talking, or at least she seemed to be. Only problem was that her words were garbled and distant. Even if I knew her dialect, it'd be hard to understand over the sound of blood thrumming in my ears.

She glanced down at the fallen mushrooms, then at me, then back down. And then she did the most stupid thing I ever saw. She started tramping all over them with her feet. I reached forward, tried stopping her, but the world spun around me and the lights went out.

I was barely aware of her helping me back to the crash site, pausing to lean me against a tree while I threw up. The next thing I knew, a blanket was being laid over me. Beneath my closed eyelids, I could see the world spinning and spinning and spinning.

17

BREAKING POINT

ANNE-MARIE - 25 AUGUST

Upon waking up, I looked over to see how Killian was faring. He seemed in a better disposition than last night, sitting crossed-legged against the back wall of our shack while writing stuff down on a napkin. His back was ramrod-straight, his hand moving jerkily on the fragile piece of paper. I didn't need to catch his gaze to know this was going to be a difficult day.

Nonetheless, he looked up at me—just a brief glance my way—before returning his attention to the items in his hands. What little expression I caught from him was enough to tell me that he was angry at me...again...for whatever reason. It wasn't like I'd been expecting thanks, but still... Didn't Killian know those mushrooms were poisonous? That I'd saved his life when I'd made him throw them up?

Sometimes, the ignorance of this man astounded me. It was nearly as vast as his arrogance, which itself was comparable in size to the sea we were surrounded by. But this was our dance, wasn't it? Every time it felt like we were making a little progress, something would happen that would make him take two steps back.

Well, I was getting tired of always being the one stepping forward. You'd think that in a situation as dire as ours, sticking together would be a bigger deal than his petty sensitivities. But no, it wasn't, not for Killian. And there were only so many times I could have my good efforts thrown back in my face before I took it personally.

With my thoughts swirling and my anger simmering close to the surface, I decided that I needed some time alone today, far away from Killian. Without any attempt at communication, I walked off, spear in hand.

My anger started to dissipate once I'd put some distance between us. As I walked down the path to the beach, I started to think of how I'd begun to feel at ease on this island. This, after all, was my first big trip abroad, my first real holiday away from home, if you want to call it that. And what a holiday it'd turned out to be!

To think that before this trip, I'd only ever been on a plane once. It'd been for a school trip, a week spent in Italy visiting museums and old churches. Aside from that, I'd been abroad a handful of times, though never this far from home. This was all new to me, and so I breathed it in with refreshing vigour.

Chamoson had been my home all my life. I'd been surrounded by millions of green lanes of grapevines that thrived on the exposed mountainside. I enjoyed caring for them and they seemed to enjoy caring for me right back, going by the juice and later wine that they produced so fruitfully. I'd always liked it there. I knew every street and short-cut. I greeted all the food store cashiers by name, never had to explain to the hairdresser how to cut my hair because she already knew how I liked it. Everyone was family, living a you-scratch-my-back-I'll-scratch-yours way of life. What more could I have asked for?

We were such a tight-knit community. I knew almost everyone and almost everyone knew me—if not by name, then by sight. I was the Legrand daughter they'd seen in the vineyard shop or working in the fields. My parents owned one of the biggest wineries in the village and I'd been helping out the family business ever since I was old enough to do it. Sure, it was hard work, but I knew nothing else. I was raised picking grapes and hauling baskets in the expectation of keeping the family business going after my parents were dead. They always kind of sheltered me from learning about the outside world. Their biggest fear was that I would want to explore and no longer be part of their long-term business plan if I found something better.

Well, this trip was going to be a life-changing event. The awkward teen with family issues that'd left Switzerland was going to come back in a couple of months a changed woman. She'd be someone who'd 'seen the world'. As fraught as this journey had been, it'd also been my chance to break free from home once and for all, to get away from the cycle of work that I had found myself born into. That was my true goal for going abroad: to come back a better person who would be proud of me for exploring and leaving in the first place. After that, I wanted to move on and keep on going. There were much brighter horizons in my future beyond my little village.

Or so I thought.

Instead, I was now stuck on a desert island, taking orders from a snappy old man with an attitude problem. *Damn if this wasn't turning out to be too much like home*, I thought, readying my spear near the tide pool. Aside from a few brief moments of clarity, Killian was disrespectful, egotistical and narcissistic. His attitude was not something that was in either of our best interests for survival on this island. Every idea that I'd come up with so far had been brilliant enough to work out for our collective good, so he had no right bossing me around or lashing out at me just because he felt like it. I didn't deserve his insecurity and jealousy and I wasn't going to take it anymore. I'd stopped being a child a while ago, so it was past time I stopped acting like one.

I marched back to the cabin later that evening, five fish riding on my spear. My anger was back with a vengeance, motivating me towards a decision I'd needed to make for some time now: take charge. Either I had to take control of this pathetic, unhealthy old man's negativity or it would be the end for both of us.

I found him sitting by the fire, still trying to tie pieces of rope together in a poor attempt at making a net. Since the sun had already set and I knew what a stubborn old goat he was, it was easy for me to guess that he'd been at it all day. Not only did he have nothing to show for it, I saw that he hadn't even gone looking for berries.

I took out the piece of wood I'd been using as a carving board. I prepared today's catch and laid it on the flat surface without a word. I caught Killian looking up just before his attention returned to that mess of tangled rope that would never be a net. Then I caught another brief glance, too little emotion attached to it.

"You're not even going to thank me?" I asked, fish in one

hand, a jagged piece of metal in the other.

My question was met with no answer. Given the language barrier, it was pointless to expect one. But I felt my temper flare regardless. Every time I'd try to motion out a thankful gesture to him, he'd look at me at first like a deer in head-lights, then like I was headless—it was no use.

I finished emptying the fish, and then cooked all five of them as crispy as can be. I didn't care that Killian liked his juicy and a little undercooked. Today, it was all about how *I* liked them, given that I caught them. Mister Insufferable was going to have to take what I caught, what I cooked, and what I decided was his share. And he'd better be thankful for that much.

Later, having finally given up his netting project, Killian reached for a fish and I gave him two. I took one for myself and started munching contentedly. Before I had time to finish it, he reached for a third one, muttering some pathetic rhetoric I couldn't understand. A few choice words drifted to the tip of my tongue, but I clenched my teeth. Instead, I nabbed the final fish before that one disappeared too.

"Sure, help yourself, why don't you?" I said, my voice as scathing as I could make it. He may not have understood my words but there was no way he would misinterpret my tone.

Killian didn't seem that bothered by my attitude. He kept on eating, as if I hadn't said anything. A few seconds of this and I exploded.

"Do you not understand simple compassion for your fellow human being?!" I yelled at him, leaping to my feet. "We are in a life-or-death situation here! Stranded on a deserted island, no help coming! So of all the damned times to learn to understand and value other people... Now. Is. The time. *Now*, Killian! Because I—"

That man cut me off by leaping to his own feet and blurting out some gibberish that was alien to my Swiss ears. He looked so stupid and pointless while he was talking...as if he were making an extreme effort to get me to understand. His volume increased by the second, not rude and obtrusive but far too abusive and controlling for me to deal with. Well, I had enough fire in me to reply in kind, and within a minute we were both yelling in each other's face as the tone escalated.

Then the unthinkable happened. Killian grabbed my wrist and shouted into my face some dumb obscenities which I was glad I didn't understand. I broke out of his wrist grab by working against his thumb before using that same hand to slap him hard across the face.

That stopped his ranting cold. The anger vanished, replaced by a flaccid mask of indifference. It'd stopped me cold too, cut the wind right out of my sails and left me feeling queasy. I could have apologised. I probably should have. But I didn't.

Instead, I turned on my heel, grabbed the nearest blanket and went as far from him as I could. I laid myself down on the earth outside, near the forest path, facing the quiet frothy waves that came to die on the moonlit shore.

Had I taken it too far? I wondered while looking up at the starry sky. *If so, why did I feel so vindicated? Killian had it coming, hadn't he? His moodiness was too much to handle. He needed to be taught that lesson. But then... that look in his eyes, when I—*

I shut my eyes as hard as I could. *I should never have done that...never. And it's too late to take it back.*

My thoughts swirling, I drifted into a fitful sleep that offered little rest.

FLOTSAM AND JETSAM

KILLIAN - 26 AUGUST

I bundled half of what we had—my half!—into a bag and left without looking back. I'd had more than enough of that woman and her entitled attitude. It was bad enough that I was stuck on this God-forsaken island. Why should I have to put up with anyone as annoying...as disrespectful...as hateful and distasteful as *her*? Short answer: I shouldn't have. So I wouldn't.

The cove we'd discovered that first day was what I had in mind. With the large rock formation on the left, the evening draft wouldn't be so bad. I bet fish were easier to catch in that ensconced space. Let Anne-Marie stay on her fancy beach and dip her toes in the sand all she wanted. I was a Scotsman. My people were used to hard pebbles and treacherous footing. Maybe that's why we were so different. I was tough as rock, she was soft as sand. And ne'er the two shall mix.

It was a short trek back to what was left of the plane's tail. On the outside, there wasn't much we hadn't cannibalised save for the tail itself and one of the back elevator fins. As I walked up to it, I made a note of their size and shape, committing the details to memory for the time when I'd be building my own shelter. It couldn't come soon enough.

Let Anne-Marie keep her four walls and flat roof. Just as long as she was out of my sight and I was out of hers, that'd be fine by me. I'd build my shelter just the way I wanted it. I could come up with a system to maximise the use of my time and resources, establish a hierarchy of priorities. It'd be a sturdy space, sure, but a practical one too. Complete with storage and amenities. Yes, that sounded like the way to go about it. In a situation like this, organisation was everything. Feeling in my element at last, I walked onto the cove with gusto.

My job at Blackfriars Bank was to assess foreign teams to maximise time and resources, better the global organisation and further the employee investment's levels...all of which would help increase the company's profit margins. That kind of job required the utmost focus and dedication, along with a lot of personal abnegation. Though I was an important part of a well-oiled machine, people always treated me as the harbinger of bad news. After all, if I'd been summoned to their corner of the world, it meant that they weren't adequate and heads would roll shortly thereafter. I never once saw a welcoming face as I went from one office to the next to carry out my duties. Few were those that understood that mine was a job that had to be done, and I took considerable pride in doing it well.

This day, it seemed the tide had changed. For the first time in a long while, there would be no one to pass judgement on my actions. No one but me.

The cove was how I remembered it. A small, hidden gap in the middle of a long rock formation that coursed the length of this side of the island. It was high enough that the high-tide wouldn't reach up to the rock's roots. I set down my stuff at the cliff's base and walked up to the water. Right then, the tide was low, the waves choppy; somewhere between rough and gentle. Dipping my fingers in, I discovered the water was as cold here as it was on the other side of the island. Well, it was all the same sea, so no surprise there.

Movement to my left caught my attention. I saw the back end of an appetising fish swimming away. The sudden appearance of a large shape above the water must have surprised it. I smiled as I realised I'd been right about the prospect of an easy meal. Besides, that one had to be twice the size of the fish that'd made it into those tiny tide-pools.

Something else caught my eye when I looked up. Something blue and red and bobbing in and out of the surf, caught between the tips of two rocks and tree branches jammed there. It was another bloody suitcase, what was left of it, anyway. There was a large tear in the plastic material on the one side. But the rest of it looked intact.

"No wasting potential resources," I muttered as I went back to where I'd left my belongings. My shoes, shirt and pants joined the pile as I readied for a swim. While I didn't look forward to dipping into the freezing waters, there was no other way to reach that flotsam and jetsam. Taking in a deep breath, I walked into the surf with clenched teeth.

Goosebumps erupted all over my skin, like an allergic reaction. But coldness was just raw information sent to my brain. I disregarded it the way a tosser back home blinks away the "smoking kills" warning on a pack of fags. Determined, I kept walking into the ocean. Once I was waist-deep, I started swimming.

The current wasn't as strong in the cove as it was near the beach and it was a short swim to reach the suitcase. It was harder to tear it away from that clog of branches though. They stood out at odd angles like protective barriers, sharp and unforgiving. I couldn't lean on the nearby rocks either. The constant water and time hadn't been enough to smooth the sharp angles and cleft edges.

I wasn't up for getting cut up yet again; the saltwater stinging at my damaged palms was bad enough. I reached out with my right arm, trying for the suitcase's side handle while I used the other to keep away from the rocks I was being pushed towards.

But my arm wasn't long enough and so my fingers missed their goal. Submerging myself, I tried going at it from below. I swam into the branches, reaching up once again, forcing myself closer as I leaned into the rough bark. The branches scraped at my skin but pain, like cold, was information best discarded in these circumstances.

I pushed closer until the tips of my fingers brushed against the plastic. With the waters pushing hard against me, I couldn't help but constantly sway to the left and right of my target. That made it all the more difficult to continue holding on to the suitcase. With my lungs burning for want of oxygen, taking the damaged case out of its wooden prison was as much a struggle as reaching it had been.

While cold was information that could be ignored, its effects couldn't. My arms and legs quickly turned into blocks of ice as the swim back to the shore took the last of my strength. The wet pebbles looked as inviting as a comfortable bed as I heaved myself onto the shore. I would have happily laid there, taking a much-needed nap, but I knew all too well the dangers of such. It'd be just a question of what would come first: the high tide or hypothermia.

With a tired sigh, I forced myself to walk to the dry clothes I'd left behind and put them back on. It was impossible to keep the tremors out of my fingers, which is why I gave up trying to zip my fly or button up my waist. *Warmth*, came the involuntary thought. *I need warmth*. It was the only thing that was going to keep the blood running through my veins, so I hugged myself hard, breathing in and out slowly.

It took long minutes of lying down, curled up in the foetal position, for strength to return to my abused limbs. I didn't dare sit back up until I'd stopped shivering. It took longer still for me to gather the necessary energy to pry open the suitcase. My fingers and palms both kept slipping off ridiculously often while I worked the zipper open. It was as if my body was punishing me for swimming in the first place.

A large bubble of laughter escaped my lips when the suitcase revealed its contents. Underneath a pile of warm clothes, I found a folded tent. An honest to goodness camping tent, with the mosquito net, pegs, and everything. I'd never gone camping a single day in my life, but I happily unpacked the thing. It was round-shaped, the size of an extra-large pizza. I laid it flat on the pebbled beach as I tried to figure out how to unfold it.

Turns out, that was as easy as one, two, three. I took the tent out of the bag it was folded into and it popped open on its own like a ballooned jack-in-the-box. The waterproof canvas was green on the sides, orange on top, and about 90 inches long by 40 inches wide. I marvelled as I unzipped the double-layered door on the side. Crouching, I moved to sit inside, feeling like a child who'd made a fort in the living room. There was room between the top of my head and the top of the tent in the middle and plenty of space around me to take all of my stuff in with me.

My new home even had two windows, one in the front and another in the back. And a storage compartment to boot.

I went back out with a smile, searching for the best spot to place it. I set it near the footpath that I'd created to access the cove, pushing it as close to the rock formation as I could; that way, the water wouldn't come leaping at it come high-tide. Next, I bundled everything I'd taken from the beach and gathered it close as I placed my new home.

The bag with the medicine and lighter went inside the tent. So did all my clothes. I didn't care that my new abode would feel cramped up. I'd happily sleep in a tight ball if it meant there was room enough to keep all of my clothes dry. On top of that, sleeping in that position would keep me warm all night. The rest of the supplies and airplane parts, I piled up next to the tent's entrance.

Once I was done, I walked back outside to take a look. The sun was setting, leaving enough light for me to marvel at the sight before me. This was more than a shelter. This was an honest-to-God home with windows and storage. It was much cosier and more inviting than that shack Anne-Marie and I had bundled together on the beach. Yes, sir, this was high-tech engineering, built to withstand the harshest of weather. While I wasn't familiar with the tent's brand, it had to be good quality if someone brought on a trip to Sweden.

Take that, Anne-Marie, you Swiss Army Knife of a woman, I thought with a wry smile. *Turns out I don't need you after all.*

I moved back inside, closing up the first layer door. Heaving a sigh, I looked at the ocean through the mosquito net. I didn't care what Anne-Marie thought, I'd been right to come here. Come winter, she could freeze to death on that beach of hers. My new home would be keeping me warm and dry.

Abandoning the ocean view, I started rearranging the interior. I placed a layer of clothes on the floor to sleep on and bundled up a shirt to use as a pillow. Everything else, I packed along one side of the tent. It would help keep me warm to have the spare clothes leaning against my back during the night. In the meantime, the supplies along the length of the tent would keep my heat in while keeping the cold out.

Next on the agenda was getting food and then eating it. No fish net to use—for the obvious reason that I'd never finished making it and never had the balls to ask Anne-Marie how to make the proper knots. So I took a spear and moved to stand in the icy cold expanse of blue outside my home.

It took me all afternoon to catch one small, frail-looking saithe, but I was too hungry to be picky. I just made sure to cook it crispy in my new firepit before munching on what little flesh there was beneath the dark-grey skin. I'd catch a better one tomorrow.

Once I was done, I moved into the tent, zipped the front door and the two windows closed and I readied myself for sleep. I was a little too tall for the small habitation, but I fit in just fine if I bent my knees. Small price to pay to be sheltered from the cold night wind that had started to blow in from the water and one that I paid gladly. This wasn't the Ritz, but it would be miles better than what I'd had to be content with since the crash.

No denying that the days were getting shorter and the

nights colder. Winter was just around the corner for us, so we'd need all the heat we could have if we wanted to survive until the return of spring.

Opening my eyes to stare at the empty darkness, I considered the implications behind that last thought. We *were* considering spending the winter here, weren't we, fools that we were? And then what? All of next year? And the years after that? Frowning, I wondered when it was that I had stopped considering this situation as temporary. *We had lives to return to, didn't we?* I wondered.

That thought left a trail of blazing cold in my head. It made me realise how I hadn't thought of my position with Blackfriars Bank in quite some time. Surely they must have dispatched someone else to Stockholm in my stead? If they had any sense, they'd have hired someone new. But I knew them well enough to fear they'd gone with the simpler option of sending someone from another department. Someone like…Alan Rogerson.

I groaned. That little shit-weasel had his eye on my job for close to three years now. That'd been true ever since he'd moved from his little agency in Devon up to the London Head Office. That unctuous git was all smiles and empty promises, rarely putting in the required work. I knew he only wanted the job for the airplane tickets and fancy hotel suites that came with it. And while he'd enjoy the free amenities and empty out the mini-bars, he'd bungle mission after mission, somehow managing to charm his way out of any repercussions. It was sad to think that my legacy with the company would come down to that—a forty-something dimwit who behaved like he was still twenty.

Closing my eyes again, I turned to the side, trying to get more comfortable in the hopes of drifting into a peaceful sleep. It didn't take long for uninvited thoughts of Anne-Marie to come to me. Despite the warmth provided by the layer of clothes, I still felt...cold. It was hard to tell, but I think that a part of me longed to have my companion sleeping beside me. I found myself listening for the familiar sound of her quiet breathing. Instead, there was only the crash of the waves on the pebbles to lull me to sleep.

I tried to push her out of my thoughts so that sleep could claim me. So of course, her face illuminated the darkness behind my eyelids. It was wearing the same look she'd had when I left. Partly hurt, partly disbelieving, and oh-so-very cross. Damn but that woman had a mind like a bull. *She'd brought it on herself though, right?* I thought. *Yes, she had. She understood what I wanted to do. She could have come with me if she wanted to. She chose to stay. That's her choice, not mine. I have to stop worrying about her. She's a grown woman, and not my responsibility. From now on, I have to look after myself and do what is best for me.*

I forced my brain to shut off its stream of unwelcome thoughts. I inhaled deeply before letting the air out of my lungs in a slow exhale. I had to sleep. I had a long day ahead of me tomorrow. I fancied using parts of the mosquito net to build a proper fish net. Yes, that would ease the fishing process, help save me some time. Best of all, it didn't require me to tie any kind of fancy-schmancy knots. Even now, I stood by my belief that a net was better than a spear to catch fish—no-matter what Explorer Extraordinaire Anne-Marie thought. If she wanted to spend hours on end crouched by a pool with a stick in her hand, so be it. I didn't have that kind of patience and my feet had enough of those damned icy cold waves.

And just like that, my missing companion had found her

way back into my mind again. Hell, the mere thought of her brought a tired smile to my lips. Aggravation aside, I hoped she was alright. And she was safe. And she was—

My mind stopped dead in its tracks, breath caught in my throat. When had I started caring? Did I...did I actually miss her?

"Yer heid's full o' mince," I scolded myself, but I knew it was too late for such recriminations. It would seem I'd learned something new today. Anne-Marie may get on my last nerve regularly, but loneliness was far worse.

AURORA BOREALIS

ANNE-MARIE - 27 AUG.-11 SEPT.

Living off fish and berries was quite easy, although very boring for the most part. The repetitiveness of the actions was beginning to annoy me. Wake up, collect dew water, pick the berries, wait for the tide pools to fill, get a fish. Wait until the day ends to cook. And then eat. And then go to sleep. Rinse and repeat.

I contemplated adding to our shelter, making it more comfortable somehow, but decided against it. For me, it was enough as is. Our shelter...I kept calling it that, even though it was solely mine now. Was it because Killian and I had built it together? Or was it because I hoped that grumpy old man would come back soon? But a week passed and then another. No sign of his return.

Nothing had changed; except, everything had. I was alone now, truly alone. And there was little doubt that winter was coming. The signs were everywhere if you took the time to look for them. The fish were starting to get scarce, the berries I once loved and cherished fated to freeze. And that was inevitable for every other piece of vegetation this island had to offer.

The only thing that hadn't been frozen was my anger and bitterness at Killian. How could he be so stubborn as to leave me like this? How was it that, in a life-or-death situation like the one we found ourselves in, he chose separation rather than togetherness? Togetherness meant warmth! And soon warmth would mean life! Had he not known that? Or was he just too far removed from his common sense to care? Either way, the frost was on the way, with the snow not far behind.

As I looked at the bare berry bushes one morning, I was tempted to curse and scream. But I held it in. What was the point in throwing a tantrum when there was no-one to see it? But damn, it was getting so cold and it was only mid-September. How much colder would it get? Was it a fools' hope to think we could make it through the winter on this island?

I made my way back to the shelter under a beating rain, wondering what other options were available. I'd long since internalized the fact that no one was going to come and save us, so we would either find a way to survive the winter or build ourselves a way out of here. But that meant building a boat, which we didn't have the material for.

Looking at the agitated water in the distance, I tried imagining how big a raft we'd have to build to make it past the wave barrier. It'd need to be a large structure: heavy enough to keep from toppling over, but light enough to float. Manoeuvrability would also be an imperative, which meant figuring out both propulsion and steering.

Looking at the pathetic excuse of a shack we'd spent weeks building, I had no choice but to admit we also lack the knowledge to risk it. We'd just have to wait out the cold.

The next morning, I woke up to a thin blanket of white sparkles on green leaves. Frost covered every visible inch of grass and leaf alike. A cough racked my lungs at the sight. I could feel my nose was clogged up. It must have been an exceedingly cold and bitter night. I wrapped a blanket around me, even though I was wearing two layers of clothes already. If only things weren't so damp all the time.

It was safe to say that summer was well and truly over, my shivering proof of this reality. I realised that I needed to warm up on a much larger scale, so I decided to start my morning off with a quick jog. I ran the length of the beach at a steady pace, overextending my arms and legs alike. I did my very best to get the blood pumping, flooding its warmth to the extremities of my body.

When it came to Mother Nature, cold was one thing not to mess with, so I pushed myself a little harder as I jogged back to my starting point. The warmth was beginning to come back to me, my heart pumping in earnest now.

I stopped near the shelter as I fought to get my breathing back under control. The morning breeze hit me in the face as I stared at the raging sea. I felt so lonely. This was the first time I had felt truly alone on this island.

More than ever, I missed my home and my family. To think that I'd come to hate that place where nothing ever happened—oh, how I wished I could go back to it now. But I knew that if I did, I'd return a very different person. It was as if I had become a new version of myself, hopefully a better version. If I'd never woken up on this island, I would never even have known of—let alone tapped into—the reserves of strength I had dormant in my bones and blood.

Upon reaching my new home, I thought of Killian. Yes, he was insufferable at times. I still missed him. Our fight had been stupid and there was no way that we could spend the winter apart. There was strength—and warmth—in numbers. So if the temperatures got much worse, I'd have to go and find him.

Later that day, as I bundled myself in the foetal position for warmth, a green essence twinkled above me. It humbly made itself known at first before rippling across the night sky in a massive wave that encompassing every angle of the deep blue-back atmosphere. The Northern Lights...they were a spectacle I'd always wished to behold. Now that I was enraptured in their beauty, I couldn't look away, not even for a second. All that could have made this moment one hundred times better was Killian being here with me and seeing them too. I'm sure they would have put a smile on his grimacing mug.

I drifted off into a peaceful slumber, my mind and dreams reflecting the dynamic dance of the emerald lights over the island.

20

THE MIRRIE DANCERS

KILLIAN - 11-17 SEPTEMBER

Seeing the Northern Lights again reminded me of home. Not the fancy loft I'd rented in Inverurie, but the country cottage house in Daviot. I spent most of my holidays there as a child. My father's parents lived just outside of the village, by the forest, near a Neolithic stone circle that stands there.

The *Loanhead of Daviot Stone Circle*, as it was called, was just a bunch of 4000-year-old rocks. Sure, the spot offered a nice broad view of the countryside to the north and east, but aside from that, it was just a dozen rocks put in a circle being eaten away by time and seasonal frost. The north-east of Scotland was very rich in stone circles and other Druidic remnants, and so our circle put the tiny village where my grandparents lived on the tourists' map. Not coincidentally, it also helped keep the village's only pub in business.

We'd often walk up there with my grandmother. She'd tell me tales of old, how the residents of the area used the interior of the circle to bury the cremated remains of their dead.

A chill ran through me at the memory, making me return

my attention to the sky above. I couldn't remember when I'd last seen the *Mirrie Dancers*, as we Scots call the Aurora Borealis. It must have been some forty or fifty years ago. Grandma Gordon used to say they were like bad omens, a manifestation of dark spirits setting the skies ablaze. That grim thought remained with me. While others marvelled at the Northern Lights, I'd always looked at that strange, eerie display with mixed feelings.

I sighed as I took in the haze of yellow, green, and purple looming over the cove. If this was the herald of bad news, the dancers were a month and a half late. I smirked, thinking that maybe this island was so remote, that's how long it took for them to deliver the bad news.

The smile faded as more thoughts drifted back to me, long-forgotten—or so I'd thought. She'd been an odd one, Grandma Gordon, but then, she *was* part of the House of Gordon. Apples never fell far from the tree in that family. And some tree that was, with roots that ran wide and deep and going as far back as 1200AD and King Malcolm III of Scotland.

I grew up listening to tales recounting the Clan's glorious past. It always started with the exploits of George Gordon, 4th Earl of Huntly, his men defeating an English army at the Battle of Haddon Rig in 1542. Then came the ghastly story of the banquet at the Forbes's Druminnor Castle in 1571, where twenty Gordons were killed. Of course, that one was always followed by the retelling of another massacre, this time of twenty-seven Forbeses of Towie at Corgarff Castle. No crime against the Clan ever went unpunished.

And on and on the history went. I remembered a painting of the brave George Gordon, 2nd Marquess of Huntly, who led Clan Gordon to victory at the Battle of Alford in 1645.

I'd read the tales of the fierce regiments of clansmen who fought the Hanoverians in 1745.

I knew Father met with the current head of the Clan, the 13th Marquess of Huntly, several times. But I'd never had that privilege...not that I'd ever wanted to. Scotland wasn't what it used to be and neither were the clans. The blood of our forefathers had ensured the lines endured, but any nobility of their actions or reasons for their sacrifices weren't so much mentioned while the gruesome tallying of their body counts kept going on and on.

For all his prancing and prawning, Father got very little out of his meetings with the Marquess. I don't know if he was hoping for a title or some land. I *do* know that he got neither. I may have been to blame for some of that. Surely it wasn't coincidental that his first meeting with the Marquess was mere months before my 18th birthday. Though he never said anything to my face, I have little doubt that Father was trying to secure me an advantageous marriage.

Just like it was no coincidence either that, during that same year, I secured myself a life well beyond his reach. My first job was with a British bank that had offices in Manhattan in the USA. As soon as I heard there was an opening there, I was on a Pan Am flight to New York. I'd been bouncing round the globe ever since, never spending more than a couple of weeks per year on my forefathers' land.

As a result, I never married, never gave my father the long-awaited male heir he'd been pining for. Another failure for him, which he added to the long list of reprimands and resentments he had against me.

The Gordons had fought on through the centuries, mighty warriors leaving behind a legacy to look up to. And all of that for what? What had it all culminated into? Just an old man on a deserted island without a hope of being found.

Two days later, I woke up with a sore throat. As the cold took hold of me, it only got worse. A strong fever weakened my already battered body and so I spend several days in a haze. I found myself caught between hallucinations and haunting dreams, hopes clashing with fears, dreams mingling with nightmares.

Unable to hunt, my food supplies started to dwindle by the fourth day. Not that I felt that hungry, but starving yourself when you're this sick is never good. Half asleep, limbs aching and trembling, I tried climbing up the path to reach the forest in the hopes of finding some edible mushrooms or berries. I went a grand total of three steps before I twisted my ankle and fell to the forest floor. Just to add injury to more injury, I cut open my left hand on some rock in the process.

I rolled a spare shirt around the wound and spent the rest of the day cradling it against my chest. I kept alternating between sleep and slumber, suffering through cold chills and feverish sweats. I would have kept within the tent for another day, but thirst got the better of me. A night spent coughing and sneezing had left my throat raw. I'd have hacked off a limb for some warm tea and a dollop of honey. As it stood, I had to make do with what little rainwater the buckets and jars I'd placed near the tent had collected.

After filling up an empty bottle to the brim, I turned to walk back to the tent. I damn near coughed up a lung as I stood back up. Before I could go inside, something caught the corner of my eye. A man was standing in the bay. Though he had water up to his knees, he didn't seem perturbed by the cold.

Every single part of me wanted to get back to the warm cocoon of clothes and blue and yellow blankets I had in the tent. Back to sleep and forgetfulness, far away from the biting wind. But I couldn't move.

The man's outline was familiar. It should have been. I'd known that tall, rigid silhouette the instant I'd laid eyes on him, even though he was facing away. A cough later, my feet started walking on their own. One step, then another, then yet another towards that man I knew couldn't be there. I blinked hard, once, twice, four times…and the man was still there, impossible though it was.

I'd stopped just shy of the waves' reach when my father turned towards me. He levelled a gaze at me that could freeze the ocean itself. He was the same as the day I'd last seen him, a little over six years ago.

It was at my cousin's funeral. Gerard had died at the age of forty-eight from pancreatic cancer. He was gone four months after first hearing the diagnosis. If it'd been anyone else, I wouldn't have come, but Gerard and I had been close when we were kids. Our parents had lived on the same street. As soon as his mum deemed me old enough to look after him, I'd take the little brat on hour-long bike rides out in the countryside. I would sit on the saddle and hold on to the handlebar grips while Gerard sat on the rear luggage carrier, holding onto me tight. The feeling of his tiny arms, just large enough to encircle my waist, was strong as I entered the church. His delighted cries of, "Go faster, Killian, go faster!" echoed with my every step.

I stayed near the back of the church for the service,

making a point not to sit in the same aisle as my father. That way, I could do my best to ignore his presence as the ceremony went on. That was the very reason I'd showed up at the last minute, betting on the first couple of rows to be full.

But I hadn't been able to avoid a run-in with my father later that afternoon. The mourners had gathered in the nearest pub; we couldn't miss each other in that cramped up place. That tends to happen when you were the only two people who were a good head taller than anyone else.

The gaze he'd pinned me with then, it was the same one he was aiming at me now. Not an I'm-happy-to-see-you gaze, but an oh-so-you-dared-to-come-after-all kind of look. It was the type that made you feel like you had to apologise for something, even if you hadn't done anything wrong.

"What must I be sorry for this time?" I heard myself asking, in a rough, strained voice. Father's eyebrows drew closer as he frowned at me. Disappointment...that was always his sign that I was supposed to know the answer to that question already.

A large burst of wind came at me from the ocean. Though I was covered in sweat, I shivered. I'd never felt so miserable and weak in my life. But proud old Rowan Gordon didn't move, didn't show an ounce of compassion for his sick son. He remained motionless, like he was waiting for me to say what was expected.

Vision swimming, head pounding, I clutched hard at the plastic bottle I held in my hands. The answer eluded me. I didn't know and I said so, mumbling the words as loud as I dared.

I knew the instant the words left my mouth that it'd been the wrong thing to say. My father's lips turned down in a nasty sneer as he took a step closer to me, his right hand rising. I knew what that meant. I'd always known what that meant.

Suddenly, he was looming over me, his adult figure large and imposing, impossibly tall to my child's eyes. We weren't on the beach anymore, but standing in the living room of our old Inverurie home. Instead of corduroy pants and three layers of shirts and sweaters, I was wearing jammies with green dinosaurs on them. But the sneer on my father's lips... that was the same. As was the burning pain on my cheek.

I reeled from the blow, knees buckling. Where my fingers expected to find the cold hardwood floor, they found wet pebbles. The thunderous waves called for me, rumbling ashore as they swirled about my feet. They urged me to follow them in their return to the sea, luring me into their depths and mysteries with promises of safety and care.

A strong bout of coughing blinded me for a moment, forcing me to close my eyes. When I reopened them, the waves bobbed flatly to the far horizon ahead, their fury abated for now. I was once again alone, deserted by every-thing and everyone, even my ghosts.

I made it back to the tent by crawling on all fours. I fell inside, lacking even the strength to zip the door closed. Just before sleep caught me in its nest, I found the answer to my father's question. *Everything.* That's what I had to be sorry for...everything.

The next time I awoke, a storm was brewing. And cold water was lapping at my feet.

21

BAD OMEN

KILLIAN - 18 SEPTEMBER

Two things struck me as my eyes flew open. Night had turned to day and there were several inches of water inside the tent.

I pushed the covers to the side and bolted outside as fast as I could in my bedraggled state. I found clouds hanging low in the sky, dark and menacing. If the clouds' darkness and the surrounding yellowish hues were anything to go by, they were minutes away from bursting, showering the island in yet more damp rain.

The skies weren't the only thing that were menacing. The ocean was in a fluxing turmoil, angry waves coming up the cove high and fast. As I turned around, I discovered that they were leaping at the rocks from all sides. There wasn't a single part of the cove that wasn't underwater.

The rock formation that had protected me all these days now served as a funnel to allow strong winds to come in from the large body of water. The gusts relentlessly pushed and pushed at the high-tide waves until they came crashing at the back of the cove. The frothing water stole whatever they could as they scurried back to the ocean proper.

My water buckets were gone. So was some of my fishing gear. If I was lucky, I'd find it floating in the cove the next morning. If not, who knew where these currents would carry them next.

The only reason the tent was still there was because I'd been in it, grounding it with my weight. The minute I stepped outside, it'd started floating and dispersing its contents of blankets and clothes into the waters. To make matters worse, the red and blue suitcase—and the lighter, knife and what little medicine I had left within—was already floating several feet to my left. With the sea churning, there was no time to get both. And it was no choice at all. I let go of the tent so I could reach for the suitcase.

Carrying the suitcase out of the cove was difficult in the low lighting. The small footpath leading away from the shore was narrow, making it slow and treacherous going. The first drops of water hit the plateau at the same time I did. Already drenched and exhausted, I sat down and placed the suitcase beside me, watching the icy drops pelt down on the world around me. There was no hiding from the rain anymore.

The wind wasn't weakening as the sky darkened. As a result, it got harder and harder to make out the green and orange canvas of the tent's canopy as it was being pushed away. The raging ocean eventually swallowed it whole, leaving me homeless.

Laughter bubbled up in my throat at that last thought. Hadn't I been more or less homeless for most of my life? Living out of airplanes and cheap hotel rooms whilst I moved from country to country, office to office? Technically, yeah, I had a flat in Inverurie. But I spent so little time there, I wasn't sure why I bothered to keep it at all. Now that flat had been empty for months, I wondered how long it'd be before someone noticed my absence. The rent payment process was automated, so I guessed it would take my bank account running dry for someone to figure it out. I was a living ghost in my own life and nothing more.

After all, what did I live for? Expectations I could never meet? My late father's approval that I knew full well would never come? All that time wishing for someone to find us, hanging onto life in the hopes that tomorrow would be the day we'd be rescued? And even if it came, then what? What was waiting for me back in the world I'd left behind? More pain, more travel, more...loneliness?

A lifetime of spreadsheets and numbers, of hotel bars and breakfast buffets, surrounded by people who feared me because they knew my coming to their office was a bad omen. A life spent putting as much distance as I could between me and the place where I'd grown up. Was *that* what I wanted to go back to, then? A life that could literally fit in a briefcase?

I'd never believed in any kind of afterlife, but if such existed, if there was an 'after', then Rowan Gordon had to be laughing his arse off now. Here was the culmination of his useless son's life: sitting at the edge of a cliff, stranded on a deserted island, long forgotten by the rest of the world, alone and drenched to the bone. I'd become the failure he'd always believed me to be. It killed me inside to have to admit to such.

I could almost see his shadow, there in between the birch trees. His dark and sunken eyes, deep under their heavy eyebrows, looking down on me. Always looking down on me, with a sense of reproach in them. Nothing I ever did was enough for that man. *I'd* never been enough.

"Well, there you go, Father," I muttered to the emptiness. "Right all along. You happy now?"

Tears mingled with raindrops as I walked back down to the cove. The pebbles creaked and rolled on their sides as they slipped under my shoes. I kept walking into the ocean, intent on not letting anything stop me. I'd never had the courage to do anything that mattered. But I did now...I had the courage to end it all. That would have to be enough.

The water lapping at my legs was freezing, same as ever. But I pushed the thought away as I kept going. I didn't slow when it reached my shoulders, didn't stop when the next wave submerged me. I had no strength left in me to stay alive. The ocean was all too happy to swallow me whole.

22

SCABBED KNEES

KILLIAN - 18 SEPTEMBER

It would be my blasted luck that the island had other plans for me.

Currents were pushing me back to the starting point. Strong and relentless, like an invisible hand determined not to let me succeed in my endeavour. They rolled me backwards, spinning me like an out-of-control Ferris wheel.

Rock formations attempted to block my path but the waves didn't stop on their account. They kept pushing me further and further until they could toss me over the rocks. My arms, legs, and back scraped and scabbed against the sharp edges. I tried screaming, but the water swallowed the sound just as it'd swallowed me. And it kept on pushing.

The cold northern winds hit me hard in the face when I broke the surface, carrying me the last couple of feet to the shore. Tears mingled with the water running down my cheeks. Blood and salted drops dripped on the cove's pebbles. I looked up to see I'd landed a couple of feet left of where I'd gone into the water.

Spent, I lay there on the pebble-covered ground, rocked

by the receding tide. Cold water ran up my legs, coming to the small of my back. Christ, but I felt miserable. More miserable than I'd ever felt in my life. Now I truly had failed at everything.

As I tried to breathe, I noticed rays of sunlight coming in through the clouds hanging low in the sky. One hit me in the face until a shadow came between me and it. I cowered in fear, my reaction instinctive. It was the shadow of a very familiar man, built like me—or maybe it was me that was built like him. Tall and lanky, grey hair and cold eyes. Them eyes were a pale shade of blue, like winter's mist. They narrowed as my father looked down on me with a mix of disdain and contempt.

"Go away," I muttered into the pebbles before he had time to open his mouth and tell me how much of a disappointment I was.

The pebbles crept under his feet as he came closer. The stench of his cologne mixed with single malt Bowmore engulfed me.

"You're not worthy of my name," he said, Scotland ringing out loudly with every vowel.

If I'd had the strength, I would have recoiled from the words. As it was, I just lay there, unable to move. Unable to defend myself, even though a part of me knew he wasn't here. Hallucination or not, the ball of lead that'd settled in the pit of my stomach felt real enough. How weak and pathetic was I? Maybe Daddy Dearest was right. Anne-Marie certainly would laugh if she could see me. I bet she'd never let anyone talk to her that way. *Naw*, that lass'd fight back, tooth and nail like an unhinged harpy.

Anne-Marie... Thinking of her uncoiled something within me, making me take a deeper breath. This time, I only smelled the aromatic ocean spray in the air. Smart, resourceful Anne-Marie, who'd taught me how to fish and cook. Funny, aloof Anne-Marie, who never understood a word I said but always got the message anyway. Strong, wilful Anne-Marie, who kept on going, no matter what this island had to throw at her.

Words danced near the tip of my tongue, a sentence that I'd never had the courage to say aloud. A statement that I'd thought of millions of times, but had yet to pass my lips... until then.

"I hate you," I muttered to the shadow that sunshine was starting to pierce through. There was no answer, just the gentle caress of the wind. Blood kept mingling with sea water while the last of my strength ebbed out with the tide. I forced whatever power I had left into my voice and screamed to the sky, God and anyone else who was listening my final declaration. "I hate you!"

23

WORDS LOST ON THE WIND

ANNE-MARIE - 19 SEPTEMBER

Rain was pouring down on the island, hard and fast. I watched as puddles started forming in the sand in front of our shelter...*my* shelter.

Not for the first time, I wondered what Killian was up to, if he was alright. I hoped so.

Two truths and a lie... Annoying as he was, I missed him. I was glad for the rain that made it easier to fight the impulse to get off my backside and go look for him. I never wanted to see him again.

I felt my lips curl up in the beginning of a smile at that joke. Renewed worry smothered that burgeoning spark of humour before I had the time to chuckle. I ought to have berated myself for that, but reproachfulness was another feeling I couldn't muster.

Life was hard and cruel. I only had to look around if I needed a handy reminder. But...life wasn't meant to be lived alone, was it? I knew I shouldn't feel that way, but I was too soft for my own good. I could never hold onto a grudge, everyone would say. I 'forgave too easily' they would mutter with more than a little despair. But there was a part of me that held onto the belief that there was something good in everyone. One only had to look deep enough.

If only Killian had let me.

If only I hadn't let him go.

When the rain broke in mid-morning, I zipped up the winter jacket I'd put on to fend off the cold winds that had picked up. Intent on going out for a morning run, I left the safety of the shelter to move out on the shore. There was a surprise waiting for me there. It froze the air in my lungs and made my heart skip a beat.

I stopped at the edge of the sand, paralyzed on the spot as my eyes made out a familiar silhouette clad in jeans and windbreaker. I felt a smile creep upon my face, my feet walking towards the shape of their own accord. They started moving at a quicker pace, carrying me to Killian, not slowing down until I was within reaching distance.

My friend was back—or rather, the ghost of him was. Up close, I could see how miserable he looked. Sickly, thin, older and undeniably frail. At some point after he left, he'd stopped attempting to shave, but the messy, grey beard wasn't enough to hide the hollow cheeks and dried skin beneath.

My arms were around him before my brain had time to form the thought. It wasn't a surprise that he hugged me back. Just like that, I couldn't remember what we'd even fought about. Whatever it was, it must not have been that important.

Long minutes later, I let go of him far enough to force him inside the shelter. He was shaking hard. Whether from the cold or something else, I didn't ask. I reached for a blanket and placed it around his shoulders. He bowed his head in acknowledgement.

I could see that a lot must have happened during our time apart. A part of me was curious to know more about that, but I didn't have the words to ask, and perhaps now wasn't the time anyway. I reached for one of his hands instead, half expecting that he would pull back, snort or do something else derisive.

He did none of these things. His trembling, cold fingers curved around mine as he returned the gesture. The grip with which he held it was tight. Though his words were lost on me, there were tears in his eyes as he spoke. Their meaning was clear enough.

24

FIRST SNOW

ANNE-MARIE - 20 SEPT.-16 OCT.

As time passed, Killian and I learned better to understand one another. We could not risk getting into another dispute like that again. It would be too much for either of us to handle. He was already starving and shivering to death in his skinniness, and I didn't have the heart to bear the loneliness that'd come from losing him. Speaking of my heart, I think the one thing that'd saved me it from shutting down was jogging. My morning runs were what got blood pumping throughout my system, let me think. Of course, the blood went to my brain that much more easily and willingly after a good run, which made thinking easier.

It got colder as the days went on. Killian wore layer upon layer of the men's clothing we'd found in that first suitcase. Eventually, he had to add some of the women's clothing on top of that just to keep himself warm. At least the rain didn't come as often as before. Still, dampness hung heavy in the air, seeping into us and chilling us to the bone, no matter how many layers we put on.

On the day it began hailing, I knew the snow wouldn't be far behind. By then, we both had realised that we had to work more on our shelter's insulation. We used whatever wood and dead leaves we could find to patch up any holes that let in a draft. But since the cold came up from the ground itself, I couldn't get warm anymore, regardless of how much grass and leaves we piled up at our feet.

Two days later, the snow finally fell on the island. We awoke on the brink of shivering under our respective piles of blankets to discover that icy diamonds blanketed the entire landscape in an eggshell white cocoon. Mother Nature was proving relentless in her attacks, but we did what we could to fight her off.

Since there were fewer fish, we learned to eat slowly, savour the food as it went down. We'd always hunted for the right amount of food needed for a meal, never taking more. But our dwindling supplies forced us to reconsider. Given how few and far in between the fish had become, they must have been hibernating or dying or whatever it was that fish did in wintertime, so we took to hunting as many of them as we could on the rare days where they showed themselves. We buried the extra rations in snow mounds.

We kept a generous stack of firewood ready at all times, storing some of it inside the shelter to dry. By mid-October we had a fire going day and night. Survival meant being prepared. That meant being meticulous, ready, consistent and steady.

As bad as this autumn was, winter still wasn't here yet. I was certain this island had more to throw at us; Mother Nature hadn't unleashed all of her furies on us yet. I began to fear we wouldn't survive it when she did.

What would we do when there was no food left? When the snow wouldn't melt for days on end? Truly, how could we ever have been so foolish as to think we had a chance?

25

ARCTIC COLD

KILLIAN - 17-31 OCTOBER

As the days went on, as we two—the odd surviving pair of acquaintances—went along on our not-so-merry way, the hours grew longer and colder alike. Nights ate at the days like the cold ate at the warm. We soon came to the realisation that there was nothing left for us here. This damn rock was sinking. Not literally, of course, but by way of freezing over. Neither Anne-Marie nor yours truly wanted to be here when it went down...because that would be when *we* went down.

Surviving on this island for so long had been no meagre feat. I'd hate to see our dignity, perseverance and diligence go to waste after all that. We'd been stupid to have wasted this much time in the first place. Then again, was it time wasted or time spent surviving? I couldn't tell the difference anymore.

Either way, one fact did remain, the sole one we'd been able to rely on since we woke up next to the tail: no one was coming for us. It'd been months now. We'd both grown weary, tired and defeated, in the very worst sense of those three words. We didn't have a prayer of making it through this winter. Half the tide-pools were frozen by now, and it was nigh unbearable to have to walk into the sea, spear in hand, to catch something. With the constant snow and no more food left, we'd only be able to survive...what, a week? Maybe two, if we were lucky?

The time had come for us to leave this island. Hell, it'd always been time to leave, but we'd wasted hours—days, weeks, even—on survival tactics and stupid, stupid arguments rather than trying to get off this hellish rock. Well, no more of that.

Agreeing on our next course of action was no discussion at all. Neither of us needed words to reach the same conclusion. Thus, we began promptly, Anne-Marie and I, to build a boat. It'd have to be big enough to fit the both of us and whatever equipment we'd need to make it back home or wherever we'd be going. It'd also have to be resilient enough to withstand the waves, which could get to colossal sizes out there. Finally—and this was the tricky part—it'd need to be made with what little material we had on hand.

Suffice to say, that left Anne-Marie and I in an ocean of a mess. Nevertheless, we started sketching out the details for the raft that would hopefully save our lives.

We ended up stripping most of our shelter apart. The fused triple panel roof made for a perfect hull from which to build. The last two months had more than proven it to be the most waterproof material we had to work with. We stripped the linings out the sides of our shelter as well, covering all the holes in the bow with these strips. There could be no mistakes, so we double-checked everything to be sure no water could get in.

Since we couldn't sleep in the shack anymore, we made

our way back to the crash-site, bedding down in the dilapidated tail-end of the plane. When it came to insulation, it was just about as barren as the shack, but it was the best we had so we huddled closer than we were used to at nights, finding warmth from the only place we could.

Despite the many layers of clothes, despite the constant fire blazing nearby, despite having a roof above our heads and despite the other's warm embrace, we froze and shivered our way through those long, cold, arctic nights. Truly, we could not leave soon enough.

26

FIGHTING ON

ANNE-MARIE - 17-31 OCTOBER

The weather showed us no mercy—not that we expected any at this point. As we worked on our raft, the island threw everything it had at us. Rain, drizzle, gale, frost, you name it, we caught it. We didn't let any of it stop us, carried on despite it all. Despite the pain and aches in our bodies. Despite the bouts of fever and sore throats. Despite the fear and loneliness that gnawed at us both constantly.

Two weeks later, our raft was nearing completion. Our resources were more strained than they'd ever been before. Our stomachs were like constant black holes. The fire we kept going was our only glimmer of hope; that and the craft that would hopefully help us escape.

The deck above the bow was made from tree branches. We'd used one of the tail's elevator flaps as a fin keel to keep us steady at sea...as long as we were steady too. In our current state, I didn't think that was a guarantee, but because we had no better option, we kept going at it.

We'd entertained the idea of having a mast and a sail, which would have given us some leverage and direction. But our ship was just too small to sustain that kind of additional weight. I created some oars out of branches and suitcase coverings, just about the perfect size and shape for this voyage to my eyes. Killian obviously thought otherwise, as he cut into them to make them look much more hydrodynamic. Before, we'd have argued about that kind of move. Now, I just gave him a thumbs up in reply.

The finished boat was so small, it barely deserved the label, so I chose to refer to it as a raft. It was large enough to accommodate the two of us, but we were going to have to let go of a lot of our previous supplies... 'a lot' as in, 'most of them'. I should have been worried by that, but I wasn't. We didn't need to take that many supplies with us. We had no intention of staying on the raft for too long. A couple of days at the most; time enough to find land, I hoped.

Hell, maybe 'raft' was too kind a name for the bunch of branches and spare plane parts we'd cobbled together. If this contraption lasted us more than a day or two without coming apart, we should consider ourselves lucky.

That left us two days, three at most, to find a shoreline. Otherwise, we'd die at sea from the cold, the hunger or both. In the privacy of my own thoughts, I prayed for the best... even as I braced myself for the worst.

27

CORRECTION COURSE

KILLIAN - 01 NOVEMBER

The open sea was something I'd always feared. I was committed to meeting deadlines, making goals for myself, reaching milestones. Out here, none of that was possible. The only thing one was able to do on a boat like ours was to sit and wait. And that was only if one was even able to stay dry. If not, all you'd be doing was treading water, waiting for the moment you'd invariably lose the fight and the depths swallow you whole. I'd already gone through that one. I knew now that I didn't want to end it like that, a forgotten soul lost in the steel blue darkness. I hoped we were ready. *We* have *to be*, I told myself. *If we not, we're gonna die.*

After we'd put the finishing touches on our raft and loaded up the supplies, we said our farewells to the island. Me, I'd have just climbed on board and paddled away, but Anne-Marie seemed to want to make this out to be much more ritualistic than it needed to be. She touched the ground with a loving caress, closing her eyes while breathing slow, deep breaths. Her voice was a soft murmur on the wind as she said, what I assumed, were her goodbyes. I, for one, was as happy as a sandboy to leave this rock. No looking back for me, thank you. But my companion had earned her moment of contemplation or whatever it was, so I stood by her side, silent.

When she looked back up to me, she had the eyes of a wild huntress. She smirked the type of halfway smile one does when they know something that you don't...but they're excited for you to see the outcome just the same. I had no idea what far-fetched thought had just crossed her mind. I had no intention of figuring it out either.

We carried the ship to the beach, walking in sync, each in step with the other, readying ourselves to embark on one last journey. I was sure if Anne-Marie could speak my language, she'd tell me, "It's not about the journey, it's about the desti-nation," or some such nonsense. Leaving our mismatched raft high enough to where the oncoming tide wouldn't get in, we started loading our craft up.

Our departure was scheduled for the very next day, at neap tide—an extremely low tide. It'd make our path off the island harder to navigate, what with the rocks closer to the surface, but it'd also mean fewer waves trying to push us back ashore, which was what we were counting on. Once we began taking notes—measuring the tides with a long, gradu-ated stick planted in the ocean—it was easy to see their pattern and the moon's influence on such. Extreme high tides happened during full moons and new moons, and low tide occurred seven days later. The full moon was seven days ago, meaning we'd have a waning crescent to look forward to tonight.

We lit a fire by the few scraps that remained of the tail-end of the Airbus. Now there was little left beyond the tail itself and the galley. Gone too was the shelter we'd built on the beach, as much of a memory as the warmth of summer. Under the crescent moon's faint glow, Anne-Marie and I shared our final supper on this merciless land mass, huddling close to one another for warmth.

I let myself lean in closer than I'd ever allowed. For once, the companionship meant more than the warmth. Anne-Marie welcomed me, not seeming to mind the close proximity as one of her arms sneaked around my back, as though it were a habitual thing. As we hugged each other by the fire, it occurred to me that my companion was no stranger to this. She was more of the touchy-feely type than I—much more, if we're being honest. But I held on, realising that I wanted this moment, needed it. It was a memory I would carry with me for a long time afterwards...provided we survived what came next.

As the night enveloped us, cloaking us in its shadows, I felt glad for the silence and our inability to talk. I don't think I could have found the words. Though I knew this was our last night on the island, it didn't really hit me until then. That's when I think I understood Anne-Marie's need to have a proper goodbye earlier. The way she'd stroked the sand so lovingly... She'd forged a relationship with this island, let it become part of her. And Anne-Marie loved herself...all of it.

And somewhere in that big heart of hers, she'd made room for me too.

I wished that I loved myself half as much as she did. But I didn't...couldn't Maybe that was my critical mistake; the one misaligned detail that derailed the entire system and that, if corrected, would allow the machine to run to its optimum capacity. Or maybe it'd help me learn how to be a better human being.

Nestled in my friend's arms, not alone for the first time in a long time, I made a vow to myself. If we got off this island alive, I would make a concentrated effort to try. I promised myself I would. As I said the words in my head, Anne-Marie held me tighter and tighter, as if she knew. I just had the strangest feeling that she did, somehow.

When night began to fall on us, I wondered if an efficiency analyst would finish his report of my character by saying, "And I believe *that* to be the ideal correction course."

28

ESCAPING THE MONSTER'S GRASP

ANNE-MARIE - 02 NOVEMBER

As gruelling as it had been, getting the ship ready was the easy part. Getting it off the island was another matter.

We'd both swam enough to know the currents were strong all around the island. They were relentless, pushing everything back where it came from. It was as if the island had a single mindset: keep us here at all costs.

We'd have to fight it, long and hard, if we wanted to get away.

The morning we took our boat to sea, we had the best conditions we possibly could hope for. A low tide, little to no wind coming from the ocean, early hours of the day with the sun a mere haze on the horizon. I'd hoped for more light, but we couldn't wait and risk the breeze picking up.

Neither of us said anything while we pushed our raft into the surf. By this point, the only words that could have helped were prayers. But I wasn't the praying type and I didn't think Killian was either.

The cold morning water bit into us but we pushed on, going as far in as we could before the water reached our hips, then we both climbed onboard. With all the stuff we'd packed, there wasn't much leg room. Killian took to the oars and I sat huddled on the left side, my weight counterbalancing the stuff we'd packed on the right.

He started rowing against the current while I kept an eye out for underwater rocks and flotsam. While rowing backwards may have sounded impractical, it was actually the most efficient technique. Boats have been rowed backward since the dawn of time, because the human body has its muscle power concentrated in the back muscles, shoulders and biceps. It makes pulling a more efficient motion than pushing, the rower less fatigued, more energy transferred to the oars, and the vessel traveling farther with each stroke.

We'd made it about a hundred metres out when the waves grew bigger and stronger. The ride no longer smooth, we could feel every high and low as we moved past wave after wave. I glanced at Killian. Despite the cold air, his brow was covered in sweat, his cheeks acquiring a rosy tinge to them. Our speed had lessened, a sign that it was getting harder and harder for him to row.

Each wave hit us like a slap in the face. It shook the raft and everything on it, splaying icy water all over the deck. By this point, I was as drenched as Killian. I shivered as I held onto the open spaces between the various floor sections, doing my best to keep from being thrown overboard. Killian was grunting as he pushed against the waves, but the island had too firm a grip onto us to readily let us go. She fought back with all the strength she had, gnawing at us, forcing us back into her fold.

The next wave almost swallowed us, tearing a scream out of Killian's mouth as he fought to hang onto the oars. When the pain distorted his face, I knew he'd reached his limits. He wasn't going to last much longer and if he let go, we were lost. Careful to keep my position and composure, I got to my knees. I had to scream his name for him to notice I'd moved. I motioned for us to switch places and he nodded.

Once I grabbed the nearest oar, I nodded for him to let go. We tried to sync our movements as I moved to the middle of the raft while he took my place. I lunged for the furthest oar as he released it, my fingers slipping on the wet branch. I tightened my grip on it, intent on keeping hold as I sat down with my back to the open sea.

Once I started rowing, I got my first good look at the island we were escaping. In the dim morning light, it felt surreal to look at. The rock formation on the left didn't look so menacing and jagged from here. The trees appeared like a small, sparse grove. The island had nothing frightening and menacing to her from this perspective. It almost seemed inviting, a deserted island getaway. For a moment, I was tempted to forget her darker, more sinister nature. But the strong current I was fighting served as a good reminder of this aspect of her natural soul. She was putting up a fight still, deploying her long tentacles as far out as she could get to get us back to her shore.

I cursed her between my teeth, trying harder and harder to put some distance between us. *Let us go!* I silently demanded, putting my back into my strokes.

"Anne-Marie," Killian called out in warning, making me look over my shoulder to see what had him so worried. The wave coming for us was bigger than any of the others. Even if I'd been standing up, it would have still been taller than me. My God, that one was going to rock us good. That was, if it didn't tear our raft in half first. If we let her hit us sideways, she was going to crush us like a twig.

I had seconds to correct our course, to position us at the perfect perpendicular angle. I put as much strength as I could muster into the oars. This was the big one; we needed speed like never before. I warned Killian to hold on fast as the wave drew closer and closer. It towered over us like a water-monster, ready to swallow us whole. When it started to curve inward, I could see the first rays of sunlight glistening on its rippling surface. I wanted to scream at the sheer horror of it. But the wind was caught in my throat, nature's last tease of a painful predicament.

The wall of water faced us and I closed my eyes, as ready as I could make myself. There was no way we could go through this unscathed.

29

ADRIFT

ANNE-MARIE - 02 NOVEMBER

I felt our raft being lifted off the surface of the ocean. I would have been sent overboard had I not been holding onto the oars. I floated in the air for an instant, before crashing back onto the deck with force. I wasn't sure why, but I kept rowing. Maybe it was because I'd been doing it so long that the motion was automatic. Muscle memory, I supposed. Maybe something was being reassured by the action.

I heard Killian scream something before the water punched me hard from behind. It wasn't a splash this time. Icy cold water surrounded me and I thought for sure we were sinking. I fought the urge to scream as I clung to the oars. An instant later, it was over and I could breathe again. My eyes flew open while I gulped down a large breath of fresh air, water dripping from my hair. The salty water burned at my eyes, but it was a small price to pay to see our raft was still afloat.

I turned back to look at the open ocean and couldn't help the laughter that bubbled up inside me. The sight that greeted me was a quiet, flat ocean that spread as far as the eye could see, melting into the azure blue of the sky far in the distance.

We'd made it… To this section of serenity, this sliver of peace, we had *made it*. I knew there was more turbulence to come, more kilometres to row. But for now, I enjoyed this calm emptiness.

I turned back and kept rowing, putting more and more distance between us and the wave barrier I could see in our wake. As the clouds parted, letting the first true rays of light beat down on us, the island looked smaller, almost humbled. She'd lost the fight.

I turned to look at Killian, found the same elation breaking through the pain and tiredness in his face. Tearing away from my gaze, I saw him look down and force himself to let go of the deck he was holding onto. His knuckles had turned white under the strain. When he looked back up at me, he had a large goofy grin that seemed to split his face in half. It looked manic beneath those large eyebrows and water-plastered hair. I couldn't hold the laughter in anymore. I released a child-like giggle that overflowed, that was too delightful even for my good.

The joy was short-lived. Killian's face darkened as fast as a brewing Northern storm. Glancing at the open ocean behind us, I couldn't see anything that'd warrant such a rapid change of emotion. I turned back to him, my eyebrows raised. He pointed to the other side of the raft. The instant my eyes set upon our stack of provisions and equipment, I understood. One of the wire-cloth cords had been torn apart clean, taking half of our cargo.

Letting go of the oars, I cursed as I moved over to check them. Thank the stars I'd packed the food and drinks at the bottom of the pile. But we'd lost everything else. The spare clothes, the blankets…the island may not have got us, but she may have sealed our fate just the same. A shiver ran through me that had nothing to do with the cold.

We took turns rowing, using the sun to adjust our bearing. Neither of us was a qualified sailor, but it wasn't like we had a destination in mind anyway. There was no way to know if we were heading in the right direction or not. I hoped we were aiming for the continent, but for all we knew, we could have been rowing towards Greenland and the North Pole. All we could do was make sure we didn't get carried back to the island we'd left so painstakingly behind us.

The day was pale and wintry, a bank of clouds hanging low and thick in the sky. Even at midday, the sun had a hard time peeking through. As a result, our clothes remained drenched most of the morning, damp throughout the afternoon. Shivering was our default mode unless we were rowing. At the very least, our frigidity gave us some much-needed motivation to row. That was the thing about nature: though her bites were sharp, the scars would always tell stories one could gather some wisdom from.

When Killian took my place at the helm, I curled in a ball on the side of the raft, a desperate attempt to preserve energy as well as a last-ditch effort to warm up. We had stored up a week's worth of rations, more if we tried fishing. But losing half of our equipment hadn't been part of the plan. Losing the ability to keep warm and change out of wet clothes changed the equation. If one or both of us got sick, we were done for.

When Killian shook me awake, it surprised me to discover night had fallen. That wasn't the only surprise I woke up to. A storm had caught up with us, rocking the raft left and right. A look up at the dark, menacing clouds revealed that they were minutes away from washing down on us.

Killian looked tired and grim in the semi-darkness. A glance at my watch revealed he'd been rowing for close to three hours. He'd stretched it too far again. I'd have given him a piece of my mind but there was no time for that. I moved to the middle of the other side of the raft, checking to see that what meagre cargo we had left remained secure. Then I took my place at the oars, ready to work.

A strike of lightning blinded us for an instant, followed by the deep rumble of thunder. The clouds opened up an instant later, washing us down in icy rain. More lightning followed. The ocean rocked us as the wind started picking up. It seemed as if it had no fixed direction to go, pushing at us from one side before hitting us with another. Or maybe it was our raft that was spinning around like a disco ball. With the clouds hiding the stars, oceans both above and below us, it was impossible to tell. All I knew is that we were right in the middle of it.

Another lightning strike hit close by, making me glad we'd taken the time to take out the heavier parts of the tail, the ones made of metal and alloy. Yes, using wood and plastic for most of the construction had been a very smart move on our parts. Lightning was a big part of how we wound up here in the first place.

It felt as if we were witnessing a contest between the ocean and sky. The thunder roared as its winds pushed down on the watery surface. The ocean gave back as hard as it got, pulsing and pushing upwards. Caught between Mother Nature's erratic spawns, our tiny raft felt like an unhinged rollercoaster cart. But there was no track to guide us, no safety bar to hold us in the vessel. Only a flimsy floor on which we rode the beasts of beasts—the ocean itself.

It was like crossing the island barrier all over again. I was paddling left and right, doing my best to take each wave upfront. Though these waves weren't as big as the ones from this morning, the rain in my eyes and dim light made the task difficult, to say nothing of the saltwater spraying up and blinding me.

Something groaned beneath my feet as we lurched to the right side, but I didn't have time to look at the disturbance. A large wave threatened to topple us from the left. I pushed on the right oar and tugged on the left, fighting to place us at that perpendicular angle again. Balance was everything.

Mere seconds later, Killian did what I couldn't do. He got to his feet and checked the bindings. I urged him to be cautious but the winds swallowed my voice.

Once we'd made it over the wave, I prepared for the next one. A glance to the side showed that Killian was trying to reattach the elevator flap we'd placed under the raft as our fin keel. It must have taken a lot of abuse this morning; it fought hard to escape. I was an idiot not to have checked on it earlier when the ocean surface was flat and there was daylight enough to see. *Well, duly noted now,* I thought sarcastically.

The angry ocean continued rocking us back and forth. I couldn't keep checking on Killian's progress if I wanted to keep my full attention on the threatening waves. I used the frequent lightning bolts to look out for oncoming threats.

Killian's voice came at me, distorted by the howling winds. I chanced a glance at him and saw that he was returning to his spot on the side of the boat. He looked defeated. I didn't need to ask what that meant. We'd lost the fin.

I wouldn't have needed him to tell me that anyway. I felt its absence the second we crashed through the next wave. My aim had been good, but the water rocked us more than it should have as we hit the wave's highest point. As it toppled over to the other side, I called out to Killian to hold on. I fought hard to keep us level. I wasn't sure, but it felt like the storm was quieting down. The lightning bolts were less frequent, the thunder more distant.

I turned back to Killian to share the good news, but couldn't find him. My arms turned to lead as my heart rate picked up. He'd been thrown overboard.

30

FLIGHT FOR LIFE

KILLIAN - 02 NOVEMBER

The water was colder than anything I'd ever experienced. I was single-malt scotch poured over ice cubes, crushed beneath them while someone shook the tumbler. Relentless waves came at me, hitting me in the face, submersing me again and again. Each time it got harder to stay afloat.

How long had I been in the drain? It couldn't have been more than a minute or two but the raft was growing already smaller in the distance. Time was but a foreign notion. Another thing crushed at the bottom of the tumbler beneath the mighty ice. A figment in the lesser sense and a God in the greater.

Swimming was out of the question. Strong waves and treacherous currents were in league against me, teaming up to drown me. As it was, keeping my head above water took all my strength. A large wave, higher than her brothers and sisters, came right at me. There was nothing I could do.

It swallowed me whole, rocking me backward into an ocean of blue and black, hot spikes of ice piercing my skin. Someone had turned the tumbler upside down, making the ice cubes shake. The impact as they hit each other was a cavernous roar.

Eyes burning, limbs on icy fire, I fought as hard as I could to return to the surface. The journey was arduous, an ordeal within an ordeal. The undercurrent pushed me in one direction, the waves in another. But I kept on fighting. Kicking with my legs, stabbing at the surrounding blackness with my arms, searching for precious air. My left arm found it and so I moved in that direction, squeezing myself through the mousse gap that led to freedom.

Air... Cold, crisp, fresh air arose to greet me. Not any warmer than its aqueous friend, but at least I was able to synthesize its energy into life. I swallowed as much as I could, gasping as it burned on the way down, much like whiskey would. I wanted to shout to the angry skies that I wasn't giving up. I'd fight on, right to the last drop.

I...I wanted to live.

After everything, I'd been through—we'd been through, Anne-Marie and I—we were worth this life and more. Something deep within me uncoiled at that thought. Freed at long last, the realisation dawned on me that I wanted to live.

What for? I had no idea. That was a question for later. For now, the thought was enough. The will was enough. And so I kept fighting to stay afloat.

The boat was far but in sight, Anne-Marie still safely onboard. She'd gotten to her knees by the side, reaching out her hand to me. Her curly hair was untied, beating down on her fear-stricken face. I could see her mouth moving, screaming my name. But the waves were fighting me back, making sure to drown out her words of encouragement.

I tried to swim to her. I truly did. But the cold was settling in, numbing everything it touched. My arms first.

Then my legs. It made every kick harder than the one before. I started to wonder how long I had until those frosty tendrils reached my heart...numbed it too.

Another wave hit me, making me lose sight of the boat again. I went under, making my lungs scream in protest, burning in their desperation for air. And I couldn't give it to them. I didn't have the strength anymore. My arms and legs had finally turned to ice.

I felt like a sinking statue, burning on the inside, freezing on the outside. It was a war of will and the fire was losing that war. I was going out the same way I'd lived most of my life. *Was this a fitting end?* I wondered. *Alone and out in the cold?*

I rather thought it was. If these were my last moments on this earth, then I wanted to take a peaceful memory with me into the void. With no effort on my part, Anne-Marie's face sprung into my mind. She was standing on the beach, dressed in that stupid chocolate aficionado shirt, a pair of too-large denim shorts, basking in a warm summer afternoon glow. Hands on her hips, head turned my way, there was an intelligent gleam behind her round blue eyes, an easy smile on her lips, always that wild mop of curly brown hair surrounding her.

Somehow, I knew with dead certainty that my friend would make it to shore. She was too damned stubborn for her story to end any other way. I found solace in the thought that she'd live on.

I'd played my part in her survival, hadn't I? Yes, I liked to think I had. I'd done my part. I'd been of real use to someone, for once. I had mattered. That was enough.

That thought I took with me as I sank deeper and deeper into the cold darkness below.

All of a sudden, my hand was pulled upwards. Shards of pain shot through my arms as they were twisted at an odd angle. Something grabbed me and pulled, and then...

Then there was air again.

Blissful, delightful, salted air. I breathed in as much as I could, as fast as I could. I choked on it, my lungs surprised at the sudden change to the point of being overwhelmed.

My sluggish brain had a hard time figuring out what had happened; my situation gave a new meaning to the term 'brain freeze'. But when my gaze settled on my companion, it all made sense. Anne-Marie was there, treading the cold water next to me. Her hair was plastered to the sides of her face whilst she fought hard to keep her lips from trembling. She had one of my arms draped around her shoulders, a fistful of the back of my jacket in one hand with a string of our cobbled-together rope clutched in the other. She looked more than determined to get a move on.

Once I nodded to her, she moved away a little to pull on the rope—once, twice—before tugging on my arm to draw me close again. The waves protested her presence. She was rigging the life and death game we'd been playing together. I smiled, realising that the waves had no idea who they'd gone up against.

Paddling to fight the currents, Anne-Marie screamed at the difficulty of the task but kept going. She pulled and tugged again and again until she had enough rope to tie around me. Then, using both hands, she yanked at the rope, even as she fought to stay afloat herself.

The waves had to know they were losing the fight, which was why they renewed their effort to drown me. They came at us hard and fast, a last-ditch effort to reach their goal. Yet

Anne-Marie never let go of that tiny rope. She kept yanking and yanking, bringing us closer and closer to the raft.

Our mismatched, dishevelled assortment of floating spare parts was a marvellous sight to behold. And a surreal one, what with the angry skies exploding above us with lightning and thunder, the waves battling for dominion of the seas and our tiny raft rocking back and forth as it fought to stay above the surf. Anne-Marie hoisted herself up first before reaching a hand down to me to grab. I reached back and our fingers clasped together.

I could feel the ocean water trying to retain me, hold onto my torso and legs, in a final, desperate attempt to pull me back under. But Anne-Marie kept on pulling, sheer stubbornness etched into every line of her young face, pulled and pulled until I was finally free.

On the uneven deck, I curled into a ball, gathering as much warmth as I could, my exhausted lungs now fighting to expel the last of the wretched water. It burned as much on the way back as it had on the way in. The rope Anne-Marie had used to save me was still tied around my torso. I saw her looping it through one of the raft's hinges before tying the other end around herself. That's when she collapsed into a heap next to me.

Her face was ashen white. I knew she had to be freezing. We both were. Icy rain still fell hard on us, but I found some solace in the thought that we were both alive to feel it. Alive and defying the elements again. Same as it *ever* was with us.

Fighting the pain of seizing muscles, I forced all the strength I had left in my right arm and reached out for her. Turning to face me more fully, she grabbed my wrist. "Thank you," I said, willing my eyes to carry the message she may not have otherwise understood.

A bolt of lightning exploded above us, illuminating the smile on her face. "You're welcome," it said in the oldest language humans knew. I pulled her close to me, huddling for warmth, remaining as one in our mutual gratitude.

Through our trauma and pain, we'd forged a new way for us to communicate. At that moment, there was no longer a need for words. Not now. Now, it was just Anne-Marie and me...and the ocean around us.

I squeezed her tightly, giving back some of what she'd given me while the chilly rain began to let up.

31

THOUGHTS OF TOMORROW

ANNE-MARIE - 03 NOVEMBER

I was cold. So very, very cold. Not to mention tired, aching, hungry and thirsty. But mostly, I was cold. And alive, so very much alive.

And not alone, I thought, curling my fingers a little more around Killian's. *Not alone*. Though his fingers were colder than mine, they gripped back.

I could feel small tremors course through them, a clear sign that he was still alive too. Alive, but barely hanging on. At this point, we were likely keeping one another alive, not with the warmth of our bodies—what little we had left—but with the electromagnetic pulses of our hearts.

That storm had quieted sometime before the first break of dawn. In the distance, the sun was rising, pale hues of red and pink reaching out through wisps of mist and banks of clouds. On the flat expense of blue that surrounded us, our tiny boat of fortune kept on floating.

So much had happened, so many things we'd been through. Alone and together.

There'd been highs. There'd been lows. But always we

drifted back together. Always, we'd endured. We'd won the fight against Mother Nature, becoming survivors. Forever changed. Forever strengthened. Forever improved.

I dreaded to think what would happen now. I'd never let myself think about tomorrow and so hadn't made any plans for it. I couldn't have, not when today itself was such a fight, when each new moment had the potential to be the last. But that was a fight that had been fought successfully. Now... now, there was the prospect of a life full of tomorrows and a later.

Or a very short life of Killian and I dying of thirst on a boat surrounded by water that neither of us can drink, a rude voice in my head said. I swatted it aside. At that moment, under the shy rising sun, I chose to be an optimist. I chose to believe that we were going to be rescued, that we were going to live. A whole life. I had no idea what to do with it, but I knew it was going to be beautiful.

We'd have to go back home, I suppose. Back to where we came from, to our lives and families. Two different places, where the other didn't belong. A sad thought, that new reality.

Killian's fingers shook beneath mine. Not that we had gotten used to each other with the island life. But we'd been keeping one another alive on a biological level. If that wasn't true intimacy, I didn't know what was. I tightened my grip around his fingers. Another goodbye of sorts, like back at the island.

I turned my head to face him. His eyes were closed on his pale face. The salt had dried and caked here and there on the ridges of his skin, at the corner of his mouth. When I gripped his fingers harder, one eye flickered open, soon followed by the other.

It took him some time to focus on me. He was tired, but he fought to keep his eyelids open long enough to meet my gaze. I poured my thoughts into a silent message: "I don't want to go."

Killian blinked back at me once, twice and then his eyes closed again. My declaration had been left unanswered.

But his hand stayed in mine. His fingers around my fingers. A trickle of warmth, swimming amidst a sea of cold. Alive and not alone.

And in the pale morning sky, white birds flew towards the rising sun.

32

TERRA FIRMA

ANNE-MARIE - 03 NOVEMBER

I felt it when Killian lost his fight against consciousness. His cold fingers stopped trembling, went limp in mine.

"No, no, no, you don't," I moaned, gathering what little strength I had left to get to my knees. The ship lurched to the side, waves leaping onboard to my right. I steadied my movements, favouring caution over urgency.

I moved slowly, calculating my movements as I shifted closer to Killian's head, the deck remaining level. Though I shook him hard, it had no effect. The skin beneath my fingers was cold to the touch, shaken by the weakest of tremors now. Much like mine, his body had given everything it had. The small cloud I could see forming with every one of his exhales told me he was breathing, but the parted lips that let the air out were tinged with blue. No, not even tinged... they *were* blue. Blue to the point of indigo. That worried me.

I had nothing left to warm him up. I had packed a few blankets and spare clothes, but they went over the side with the suitcase we'd lost. I gathered him in my lap. I didn't have much body warmth to share, but I would gladly give him everything I had left.

My heart sank as he let himself be manhandled without protest. Had he been conscious, he would never have accepted such proximity and the display of weakness that it betrayed. He probably would have made dire a comment in that low voice of his. And his eyebrows would have crossed as if they were one, signalling his displeasure for everyone to see.

But as I gathered him in my arms, Killian did none of those things. He was cold and unmoving. Dying, now that we were closer to safety than we'd been in weeks.

I rubbed my hands along his arms, generating heat and friction, showing him how he was never alone, telling him to fight on just a bit more. Just a little while longer. I held onto him, praying to every God I knew, pleading with the universe itself for my friend to live long enough so someone could find us. It could have all been so simple, and yet here we were…all so difficult.

Above us, the birds had gathered in a circle. In this vast desert of an ocean, we'd captured their attention. I could guess at what they saw: two survivors on the road to salvation, or two lost souls tricking themselves into thinking they had a chance. What was it we were holding onto, hope or despair?

I had half a mind to ask them out loud when something else caught my attention. Far away on the horizon, wisps of mist parted, revealing the outline of something big and dark. I tightened my hold on to Killian as the breath caught in my throat. It was a cliff… A huge, beautiful, blessed cliff!

"Hold on," I told him, as a smile broke free on my face. "You hear me, you stupid old man, hold on."

I moved out from underneath him and shook off my coat. The cold bit hard into me as I placed it over Killian's limp form. Once I got to the centre of the boat, I reached for the oars.

Five minutes later, I couldn't feel the cold anymore. I was on fire, my arms and back burning from the strain. Every freezing breath I took fed the flames growing in my lungs. But that glorious cliff was getting bigger and bigger.

Whatever we'd reached was no small island. I couldn't see the end of it on either side. Maybe we'd hit *terra firma* at long last. God, how I hoped—how I prayed—we did.

Waves started pulling us in the right direction, making it easier to row. Our tiny embarkation gained speed. I could see a small cove ahead of us, what looked like a small rocky beach in the centre. I aimed for it as best I could. Now was *not* the time to crash into a rock formation.

As I kept rowing, elated by the proximity of salvation, my eyes settled on an even better sight. There were people atop that cliff. Mere pinpoints on the horizon at first, but they grew bigger as we got closer—a couple holding hands. A man with long brown hair beating in the winds, a beard that seemed longer than his hair. By his side, a woman with dark hair, held together by a colourful bandanna.

Out of strength, frozen to the bone, tired beyond words, I reached a hand to the sky and waved at them.

Exhausted, I collapsed onto the deck. The oars slipped out of my hands and into the ocean. Killian was passed out a few centimetres from me. I turned to face him with a smile.

"They waved back," I told him, right before the world went black.

33

MELE KALIKIMAKA

ANNE-MARIE - 25 DECEMBER

I watched with a smile as a familiar silhouette became visible on the horizon. I would know that gangly stick of a shape anywhere. Though he'd kept some of the muscle he gained on the island, Killian was as lanky and thin as ever.

The sun was rising behind him, a fiery ball of orange and red above the quiet ocean waves. Killian was almost out of the surf, walking out of the water and onto the beige sand. He wore nothing but grey swimming trunks, the colour matching the wet hair he was combing his hand through. He wore it longer these days, the curls I always suspected existed starting to show.

Leaning back down in my chair, I closed my eyes, basking in the warm glow of what was shaping out to be another day in paradise. There was a light breeze in the air, carrying with it the sweet fragrance of the plumerias that grew nearby.

Almost a year and a half had passed since the crash of Flight SWA 1528, somewhere in the Arctic Circle. It'd been almost fourteen months since we officially came back to life and reclaimed our lives, coming ashore on one of the Lofoten Islands in Northern Norway.

That lovely couple who helped us back on land brought us to a local hospital next. There, one of the nurses called the police. Less than a week later, Killian and I went our separate ways, each one of us boarding a different plane to head back to our homes, to our loved ones. Well...one of us did. It hadn't taken me long to discover that Killian didn't have much of anyone to go back home to.

Aside from a first-class flight to the motherland—that we'd been assured wouldn't crash—the airline insurance company gave each of us a large check as "compensation for the emotional ordeal we went through, the result of this tragic, unforeseen and rare accident", as their lawyer put it. A friend of my mother called it "bribe money" to make sure we wouldn't sue them at a later date. I didn't care either way. I counted the zeroes and nodded my thanks. It was more money than I could ever dream of earning. More than if I'd won the national Swiss lottery, in fact.

A large cheque wasn't the only thing our trip north earned us. It got us the fifteen minutes of fame that neither of us wanted. The "Arctic Circle Survivors" as the media dubbed us, were all over the news for weeks. The media got their hands on a professional picture of Killian. In it, he stood tall and proud, wearing a light grey designer suit, thick eyebrows frowning at the camera over steely blue eyes. His hair was neatly combed back to add gravitas to the pose.

For me, they went with a picture they harvested off the internet, one I remembered being taken on a warm sunny day where I was wearing a short-sleeved lilac shirt and an old pair of blue jeans that had been cut above the knees. I'd been out all afternoon, helping out in the vineyards. My dad had captured the moment with his smartphone, calling out to me first and then snapping the picture when I turned back to look at him. I had my hair up in a ponytail, an easy-going smile on my face. Somehow it had ended up on the family winery's website.

Seeing as Killian and I were the sole survivors of Flight SWA 1528, these two pictures made the front page of newspapers in over one hundred and twenty countries. As for the last seventy or so countries, I was told they either didn't have a newspaper or they printed our pictures in between pages two and six.

If only the rest had done that. For a little while, we were forced to stand at the centre of a media freak show. Everyone shone a bright light on us, dissecting our lives and words, as if we somehow held the key to answering life's biggest mysteries or something. To say it was weird was an understatement, but it helped me understand and realise how much the media fed on instant gratification.

Everyone wanted to hear the story of our survival. Everyone wanted to know what we'd had to do to deny death; how it felt to live in such isolation with so little resources and even less hopes of making it out alive. Then again, we also got prize questions like, "Ninety-four days without a smartphone, that must have driven you mad, didn't it?", "What was the first film you watched upon your return?" and "Have you had time yet to catch up on your social media feeds?" Not things that goes through *anyone's* mind when the struggle is over.

People everywhere were curious about the dire thoughts that must have crossed our minds as the Grim Reaper crept closer and closer each night. How we felt about each other, what our prospects for the future were, how we planned to use this second chance at life.

"Have you seen Killian Gordon again since you came back?" they'd ask. "He was all you had for close to a hundred days. What was your relationship like on the island? Did it ever get physical?"

Wealthy people came from far and wide to meet us. Their briefcases were filled with fat cheques on top of book or movie proposals. The requests for interviews on television and in the press were too numerous for me to keep track of. Everyone I knew, from my dentist to the clerk I had to speak to at the tax office, wanted to hear *the* story.

Well, to everyone's disappointment, it was a story neither Killian nor I wanted to tell. However, journalists are nothing if not resilient. Having long since discovered that empty spaces don't sell, they resorted to being resourceful. It didn't matter that we had nothing to share with them. They found words elsewhere to print on their pages, information to fill their air-time slots, websites and print columns. They went after our families and friends, talked to our colleagues and former school teachers. And surprise, surprise, at times like these, it turns out everyone and their dog has something to say.

While I had no interest in reading about my life—I was the one living it, after all—I paid attention to the stories they ran about Killian. As everyone on the planet was being fed misremembered childhood stories and bland anecdotes, I listened to the awkward stutter in the middle of too-short sentences, the long pauses between questions and answers.

I was surprised to discover Killian's colleagues had a hard time describing him. They never strayed far from the professional sphere and had nothing more profound to say than

"He was a hard-working employee who did a difficult job with ease". Journalists didn't get much further on the home front either, failing to find relatives or friends with an interesting story to tell. More surprisingly, they had yet to come up with anything resembling a former lover.

While the media struggled to unravel the enigma that was Killian Gordon, I understood what the Scot had never found the words to tell me. He was alone in this world, nothing but his job to cling to.

Soon after that realisation hit me, I contacted my lawyer for a way to get in touch with him. Later that very night, I was on the phone with Killian, stringing along words that barely sounded like English.

Even though I struggled to make sense of his replies without the visual clues I'd become so reliant upon, it felt good hearing his voice on the other end of the line. There were long pauses and silences that stretched late into the night. But it was a connection regardless. In the end, we didn't talk much—we never had, really—but we stayed on the line for hours.

It reassured me to know that he was alive and well. It made me realise how much I'd missed him, missed the companionship we'd built on that monster of an island. We'd fought it side by side to total victory. We'd crashed together and left together. Each of us had left a part of ourselves on those shores. Each of us had gained something through the ordeal. Now that we'd strayed far from the island's grasp and enough time had passed, I realised we returned home with something more than scars. We'd acquired a strength that wasn't physical, a knowledge that couldn't be shared. It was something unique that couldn't be seen or touched, something Killian and I now both possessed, which resonated within us, echoing in each pause, stretching into the silences.

That island would never forget us, no matter how hard it tried. But neither would we forget it. I felt a sense of true human pleasure from leaving a mark, one even more distinguishable than what the airplane had left on its shore. We'd left a mark of gratitude on the sand, a sign of resilience and survival.

After that night, it didn't take me long to find myself seated on a train north-bound, heading for Scotland, an *English for Dummies* book in my lap. I hadn't been able to tell Killian on the phone that I was coming to visit. Surprise trapped the voice in his throat when he welcomed me into his flat two days later.

Never had silence been more fitting. The tears in his eyes did all the talking for him. There was a sacredness to them, speaking with a similar conviction to that of the waves that almost took our lives. They understood and they remembered.

"Daydreaming again, I see," a familiar voice spoke from up-close, the words said with an even more familiar Northern accent. "You're supposed to be working."

I reopened my eyes. I glanced up from my beach chair to find Killian looking down at me. He'd wrapped a light-blue towel around his shoulders, his hair dripping salted droplets on his tanned face. Though he was trying for a stern face, I could tell a smile was struggling to break free at the corner of his lips. Wasn't this who he was, to a T? I found the expression endearing.

A glance at my watch told me he was right, though. As of two minutes ago, our little business venture was open for the day. Sitting up, I planted both feet on the ground, feeling the warm sand roll beneath my feet as I sank in a little. The feeling brought a smile to my face as I turned to the juice bar on my left.

It had been built out of plywood and bamboo sticks, decorated with hand-painted lei flowers. Moving behind the counter, Killian flicked a switch. The "Fresh Organic Juices" neon sign buzzed to life. The ceiling fan followed suit, whirring to full rotation above our heads.

From a business standpoint, we were doing better than fine. In fact, we were doing amazing. Killian's knack for numbers, strict business regimen and the logistical bend was the perfect counterbalance to my more emotional creativity. I'd come up with the flavours and recipes. Killian implemented marketing ideas before cracking down on numerical predictions. I knew that our business was young, understood that there would be bumps down the road. But those were worth driving over and handling. If the island had taught us one thing, it was that we were stronger together than alone. With a common goal in heart, mind and soul, I knew Killian and I could do anything we set our ambitions on.

Before moving to my spot behind the counter, I spared one last look at the horizon, its hues of red and blue over the golden sand. I was happy in the knowledge that this Christmas was going to be sunny, warm and spent on a lush island filled to the brim with life and joy.

We'd chosen well, I congratulated myself, not for the first time. Not only was this place bathed by an ever-warm glowing sun from dusk till dawn. It was also an island where cold was but a foreign concept, snow something so exotic that you only saw it in pictures and movies.

"Tick tock, time to open up," Killian sing-songed, powering on the plastic till seated next to the pile of bamboo cups we would need for the day.

I gave him a mock salute before flipping the "Closed" sign over so that it read "*Ouvert*", the French way of saying 'Open'.

I was pretty sure we were the only bilingual juice-bar for miles that was served by a middle-aged Scotsman and a twenty-something Swiss girl. And that suited me just fine.

I took my place beside my friend and gave him the traditional Hawaiian seasonal greeting. "*Mele Kalikimaka*."

34

TRANSLATIONS

French
Bouillabaisse: a popular type of fish soup
Ouvert: open
Sel: salt

Gaelic
An donas dubh: by the devil

Hawaiian
Mele Kalikimaka: Merry Christmas

Latin
Terra Firma: solid earth

Patois Valaisan

Âlâ piè: come on
Bôrtâ tzouze: nasty thing
L'ê môrô: it's not what you think
Vin avoui mè fira onna promenâde: come with me for a little walk
Tzantin Tzamozard: Song of Chamoson

Scottish

Aye: yes/yeah
Chitter: shivering
Cludgie: toilets
Hullo: hello
Lass/Lassie: girl
Lavvy: toilets
Naw: no
Oi: eh
Yer heid's full o' mince: your head's full of crap

35

ADDITIONAL NOTES

The *Patois Valaisan* is a local dialect of the Franco-Provençal language.

Franco-Provençal emerged as a variety of Latin; the first traces of the language date back to the 5th century AD. It was spoken in a large area that surrounded the Leman Lake and included entire regions of France (east), Switzerland (west) and Italy (north). The Franco-Provençal language started dying in 1540 when French replaced Latin as the official language of the area. Nowadays very few people even know that it once existed, and it is even worse for the local dialects.

The *Patois Valaisan* is exclusively spoken in the French part of the Swiss canton of Valais (an area of about eighty by eighty square kilometres in the Rhone Valley). It is officially labelled a dying language, as only a few of the local elderly people are still capable of carrying out an entire conversation in the language, while younger generations only know a couple of words and/or the most popular expressions.

Thankfully, there are historians and language enthusiasts whose aim is to keep it alive. While some local groups get together to speak it and teach it to those interested, several scholars have begun to document and archive the language in an effort to preserve it.

NOTE FROM THE AUTHOR

THANKS FOR READING!

If you loved this book and have a moment to spare, I would really appreciate a short review where you bought it. Your help in spreading the word is gratefully appreciated.

FURTHER READING

THE NEVE & EGAN CASES SERIES

A BOLD STUDENT. A SIGHTLESS PROFESSOR. AND A PRIVATE EYE BUSINESS THAT GROWS DEADLIER BY THE DAY...

University student turned PI Alexandra Neve leaves no stone unturned. And when her keen instincts combine with her blind partner's analytical mind, the crime-solving pair sniffs out clues others can't see. But with mafia conspiracies to crack, looted WWII treasure to recover, and captive ballerinas to rescue, the duo can barely keep up with their never-ending caseload.

As Neve and Egan's sleuthing abilities grow with each case, dangerous new crimes take them to the brink of destruction. And with the London streets hiding deadly mobs and madmen, the unlikely pair must keep on their toes... before they end up underground.

Will the two rookie PIs survive to full-fledged pros before their new calling turns deadly?

The Neve & Egan Cases Box Set contains four rollicking full-length mysteries. If you like courageous characters, puzzling plots, and non-stop clue-cracking, then you'll love Cristelle Comby's captivating adventures.

FURTHER READING

VALE INVESTIGATION SERIES

MEET BELLAMY VALE, A WORN-OUT GUMSHOE TRYING TO AVERT THE APOCALYPSE, ONE FIGHT AT A TIME...

PI Bellamy Vale's immortality is exhausting. Solving endless supernatural crimes may keep the bill collectors at bay, but the deal he made with a demon is taking a heavy toll on his mind.

Fighting back monsters from the underworld, booting out paranormal predators, and dodging dubious deities, Vale fears being able to interrogate the recently deceased wasn't worth the price of his soul. And as he doggedly attempts to do the devil's dirty work, the scrappy detective could find his ill-gotten powers aren't enough to save him from oblivion.

Can he dispatch the worst fiends of the darkness without triggering a universe-shattering nightmare?

Vale Investigation - Box Set contains the wickedly rollicking five books in the Vale Investigation urban fantasy series. If you like sarcastic private eyes, magical mayhem, and noir-style humor, then you'll love Cristelle Comby's otherworldly collection.

FURTHER READING

RED LIES

SHE'S ALWAYS FOLLOWED ORDERS. NOW SHE
WANTS OUT. THE PRICE OF FREEDOM MAY BE
HER LIFE.

Moscow, 1986. Soviet spy Sofiya Litvinova longs to end her
days exclusively working sexpionage missions. But when
she's dispatched to Stockholm to deploy her honey-trap
tactics against a suspected Russian traitor, she has no choice
but to comply. Until the assignment goes awry after the
diplomat pegs her as KGB during the attempted seduction.

With her cover blown and life in danger, Sofiya agrees to
help the man carry out his own covert mission while secretly
reporting to her superiors. But when his dangerous black-
mail agenda coincides with a devastating explosion in Cher-
nobyl, her hopes for deliverance vanish in a cloud of
radioactive dust and political powerplays.

Can Sofiya escape the agency's deadly clutches before she
becomes expendable?

Red Lies is a fast-paced standalone espionage thriller. If you like international stakes, authentic historical details, and suspense with heart, then you'll love Cristelle Comby's captivating adventure.

ABOUT THE AUTHOR

Cristelle Comby was born and raised in the French-speaking area of Switzerland, on the shores of Lake Geneva, where she still resides.

She attributes to her origins her ever-peaceful nature and her undying love for chocolate. She has a passion for art, which also includes an interest in drawing and acting.

She is the author of the NEVE & EGAN CASES mystery series, which features an unlikely duo of private detectives in London: Ashford Egan, a blind History professor, and Alexandra Neve, one of his students.

Currently, she is hard at work on her Urban Fantasy series VALE INVESTIGATION which chronicles the exploits of Death's only envoy on Earth, PI Bellamy Vale, in the fictitious town of Cold City, USA.

The first novel in the series, *Hostile Takeover*, won the 2019 Independent Press Award in the Urban Fantasy category.

KEEP IN TOUCH

You can sign up for Cristelle Comby's newsletter, with giveaways and the latest releases. This will also allow you to download two exclusives stories you cannot get anywhere else: *Redemption Road* (VALE INVESTIGATION prequel novella) and *Personal Favour* (NEVE & EGAN CASES prequel novella).

www.cristelle-comby.com/freebooks

Made in United States
North Haven, CT
31 May 2023

37202895R00146